The Adventures
of Anatole

Nancy Willard

Illustrated by
David McPhail

NEW YORK REVIEW BOOKS
New York

THIS IS A NEW YORK REVIEW BOOK
PUBLISHED BY THE NEW YORK REVIEW OF BOOKS
435 Hudson Street, New York, NY 10014
www.nyrb.com

Originally published in three volumes: *Sailing to Cythera*, 1974; *The Island of the Grass King*, 1979; *Uncle Terrible*, 1982.

Decorative letters for "The Island of the Grass King" by John O'Connor
Decorative letters for "Uncle Terrible" by Sarah E. Knowles

Library of Congress Cataloging-in-Publication Data
Names: Willard, Nancy, author. | McPhail, David, 1940– illustrator.
Title: The adventures of Anatole / by Nancy Willard ; illustrated by David
  McPhail.
Description: New York : New York Review Books, [2018] | Series: NYRB
  kids | Summary: In this collection, Anatole, usually accompanied by his cat
  Plumpet, embarks on a search for wild fennel, plays high-stakes checkers
  against a wizard, and attempts to right the wrongs in each land he visits.
Identifiers: LCCN 2018020039 (print) | LCCN 2018036006 (ebook) | ISBN
  9781681372938 (epub) | ISBN 9781681372921 (paperback)
Subjects: | CYAC: Fantasy. | BISAC: JUVENILE FICTION / Fantasy & Magic. |
  JUVENILE FICTION / Action & Adventure / General. | JUVENILE FICTION
  / Animals / Cats.
Classification: LCC PZ7.W6553 (ebook) | LCC PZ7.W6553 Adv 2018 (print) |
  DDC [E]—dc23
LC record available at https://lccn.loc.gov/2018020039

ISBN 978-1-68137-292-1
Available as an electronic book; ISBN 978-1-68137-293-8

Cover design: Leone Design, Tony Leone and Cara Ciardelli

Printed in the United States of America on acid-free paper.
10 9 8 7 6 5 4 3 2 1

For James Anatole Lindbloom, to take on his travels
and
For Jerry, who loves Shakespeare and Spiderman

Contents

Gospel Train

here was once a boy who lived with a cat. The boy was called Anatole. The cat was called Plumpet, which tells you something about her size and habits. She was fond of field mice, herring, and whipped cream, and she had stripes the color of milk and honey.

In the summer Anatole lived at Plumpet's cottage behind the woodshed. Afternoons they would sit outside under the apple tree while Plumpet knitted and Anatole played with his train and sang:

"The Gospel Train is coming.
I hear it just at hand,
I hear those wheels a-rumbling
and rolling through the land."

His papa had taught him that song and had given him, for his fifth birthday, a gold pocket watch with an engine engraved on the back. It had belonged to Anatole's grand-papa, who was once a train conductor. The hands on the watch always said a quarter of eleven, regardless of what other clocks said.

Sometimes his papa took him to the train station to watch the trains come in and out. Once the engineer of the Penn Central's nine-thirty to New York had let them ride as far as the end of the platform.

Anatole always invited Plumpet to come, too, but she refused. And she was not impressed with his American Flyer baggage car and two passenger cars, his Lionel engine and tender, his Babe Ruth boxcar, and his Chesapeake & Ohio gondola.

"What do I care about diesels and bells and water pumps?" she exclaimed. "What has all that to do with me?"

In the winter Plumpet moved into Anatole's house as there was no heat in her cottage. Other people lived in Anatole's house, too, but they are not in this story.

One spring morning Anatole woke up early and looked

out of his window and saw Plumpet under the apple tree digging a hole with a silver spade. Generally she dug with her claws. Beside her stood a black cat holding a golden box, and as Plumpet dug, the black cat sang:

> "Requiem eternam dona eis,
> Lux perpetua luceat eis."

Then the black cat lowered the box into the hole, and Plumpet filled in the hole, and the black cat bowed, shouldered the spade, walked into the honeysuckle thicket, and was gone.

Anatole hurried outside, but Plumpet had gone around to the front yard and taken a tiny stone in her paws and was crouched in a patch of mint, drawing on the sidewalk that led past the garden to the street.

Her drawing looked like this:

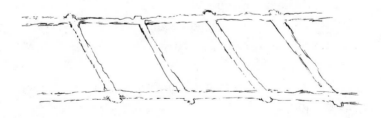

"Is it for Hopscotch?" asked Anatole.

"Not Hopscotch," said the cat.

"Tiddlywinks?" asked Anatole.

"Not Tiddlywinks, either," said the cat.

"Hop-o'-my-Thumb."

"Not Hop-o'-my-Thumb."

"What then?" asked Anatole. "And what did you bury under the apple tree?"

Plumpet drew the last rung on her ladder.

"You remember my old Aunt Pitterpat, who lived in Roscoe's General Store," said Plumpet.

Anatole remembered a black-and-white cat nestled in the sunny window among the cigar boxes. Mrs. Roscoe always had black-and-white cats.

"I remember," he said.

"My Aunt Pitterpat has gone to get a new skin. She sent me the old one to bury, and she's invited us both to her christening party," said Plumpet. "Cats have nine lives and nine christenings. This is Pitterpat's ninth. I've drawn a railroad track, so the train can find us."

And Plumpet scratched a tiny hole under the peonies and buried her writing stone.

"No trains run on Grand Avenue," said Anatole. "And we're miles away from the station."

"All things come to those who wait," said Plumpet, and she sat down on a bench that was not there until she looked for it.

A man hurried past them, pushing a baggage cart, and then a train whistle sounded, far beyond the garden. The flowers closed their petals and dreamed of a train

"ACROSS THE AISLE SAT TWO OWLS IN BONNETS. IN THE SEAT OPPOSITE
ANATOLE, A RACCOON WAS READING THE NEWSPAPER."

platform, on which Anatole now found himself standing, much to his surprise, watching the train rush closer and closer.

"You see," said Plumpet, "doubt is the root of all failure."

It was as comfortable a train as you could wish for. There was a first-class coach, with doors that locked if you wished to sit alone. There was a coach for eating supper, and a coach for playing checkers, and a coach for drinking tea, and a sleeping coach.

Plumpet and Anatole rode in the second-class coach. Across the aisle sat two owls in bonnets. In the seat opposite Anatole, a raccoon was reading the newspaper. Behind them, a mouse child's voice squeaked, "Is that Grainesville, Mother?"

"Not yet," said a deeper voice. "Soon."

The conductor, a handsome Barbary sheep, did not collect tickets. Instead, he walked up and down the aisle and called out the stops.

"Pudding Street Station! Pumpkin Lane next!"

And late in the afternoon he called out, "St. John's Meadow! Fifteen-minute stop for anyone wishing to pick a bouquet!"

When the train stopped at St. John's Meadow, everyone got off. The air was warm and sweet. Far away at the edge of the meadow, Anatole saw a family of rabbits cutting hay and spreading it on racks to dry and singing as they worked:

"O, the racing of the sun
and the rising of the moon.
These flowers green and tall
must go the way of all,
and winter comes too soon.

"O, the sparrows in the sky
and the dragons in the sea.
In mad or merry weather,
we'll take our rest together
under the apple tree."

Anatole remembered his apple tree at home, and he was so happy that he didn't feel like picking anything. Instead, he walked to the front of the train and investigated the engine. A fox in a jaunty blue cap sat in the engineer's seat. A squirrel was shoveling coal into the firebox.

"This is an old train," said Anatole to himself. "Nowadays, they have diesel engines."

Plumpet picked some catnip, and the raccoon stuck a primrose into his lapel. He offered one to Plumpet, who refused, saying she did not affect clothes.

"All aboard," called the conductor.

When the train started up, everyone took out picnic hampers and lunch boxes except the raccoon, who took out a cigar.

"Ah, dear." Plumpet sighed. "We've forgotten to pack a lunch."

The two owls, seeing their predicament, offered them three roasted mice and a small bottle of elderberry wine. Anatole could not bring himself to eat the mice, but he found the elderberry wine very good, and he drank his share quickly. Plumpet never ate or drank anything quickly. She said it harmed the digestion. She ate the mice slowly between loud purrs.

"Lovely plump little things," she said, licking her chin. And she gazed wickedly across the aisle.

"I hope you're not thinking of eating the owls," exclaimed Anatole.

"Certainly not," said Plumpet, shocked. "It's against the rules here. Where would we all be if we tried to eat each other up?"

Suddenly the coach grew dark. A hen roosting on the baggage rack tucked her head under her wing. Anatole looked out the window. The train was entering a thick forest, where presently it stopped.

"This is the border," said Plumpet. "This is where the ferryman collects his toll and carries us across the river."

"You mean the train goes on a boat?" asked Anatole, very much interested.

Plumpet yawned. "How should I know? What does it matter so long as we get there?"

The train started up again, and now water lapped on both sides of them. But before Anatole could tell how the crossing was done, they had reached the other side and entered a tunnel carved into an enormous tree.

"This is the gate to Morgentown," said Plumpet. "I should love to have a postcard of it to hang in my cottage. But nobody in Morgentown sends postcards."

When they arrived, it was twilight. ("It's never night in Morgentown," the conductor assured them.) Lanterns twinkled like low stars over the city square. Cats jostled past them on bicycles, and rabbits pulled carts piled high with cabbages, and falcons hawked pieces of sky, souvenirs of Morgentown.

"A fake," said the raccoon. "The sky sailed out of reach years ago. Good-bye."

"How shall we find your Aunt Pitterpat?" asked Anatole. It did not seem possible to find anyone here among so many. Plumpet was not discouraged.

"She sent me word to look for her at the party. She's probably riding the merry-go-round. Oh, Pitterpat was always a great one for rides. She used to jump into Mrs. Roscoe's car every chance she got."

When they came to the merry-go-round, there was Pitterpat perched on a white horse moving up and down, up and down to the music.

"Climb aboard!" she called. "This ride never stops, and the music goes on forever."

So Anatole grabbed a red horse and Plumpet leaped on a blue one, and Pitterpat rode between them.

"You're looking well," observed Plumpet. "Your new skin is the same color as your old one."

"Yes, and it won't wear out. The ninth skin lasts forever."

"Shall you be coming back to the store?" asked Anatole.

"No," said Pitterpat sadly. "Give my love to my kittens, Plumpet. Has Mrs. Roscoe found good homes for them yet?"

"I think," said Plumpet, "she's going to keep them herself."

"Ah," said Pitterpat, "I'd like to give them a little treat, but we aren't allowed to send anything out of here. But tell them I'm happy." Her voice sounded sad, but behind the sadness she was purring. "And enjoy yourselves. Don't drink too much blackberry juice. It will make you so sleepy that you'll miss the train home."

"If we miss the first train, we'll catch the next one," said Plumpet.

But Pitterpat looked grave.

"If you miss the midnight special, you'll never be able to leave. That's in the rules for visitors. If you miss the train, you must stay here forever."

"We'll be careful," said Anatole.

"One last thing," said Pitterpat. "The kittens are so fond of catnip. Do you think, Plumpet, you could plant them a little bush—"

"Don't mention it," said Plumpet.

"Enjoy yourselves," said Pitterpat.

And they did enjoy themselves. They rode the merry-go-round and the Ferris wheel, and then they went back to the merry-go-round, and then Plumpet said, "I'm starved."

"Look, there's a cafe," said Anatole. "Wouldn't it be fun to eat under one of those purple umbrellas?"

While they were sipping their blackberry juice and eating their chocolate ice cream, Anatole spied a train running round and round on a little track.

"Oh, Plumpet," he exclaimed. "Let's ride on that!"

"What? Why, we've bounced about in a train half the day, and you're ready to ride another one! Well, I can't let you ride it alone."

But she enjoyed herself all the same.

When the lanterns fell asleep and the sun came up, a pig in a long blue coat crossed the square, ringing a bell and shouting, "Last train out! All those leaving for the mainland, last train out!"

"Oh!" exclaimed Anatole. "I forgot all about the time!"

And with Plumpet at his heels, he hurried away from the party.

They boarded the train, and the conductor pulled up the stairs after them. The cars were nearly full. Plumpet and Anatole took the last seats. Then they waited for the train to move.

They waited and waited. Anatole took out his watch and studied it. The hands said a quarter of eleven, of course.

"What can be the matter?" exclaimed the raccoon.

And a turtle said, "I need not have hurried. That's clear."

At last the conductor entered the car.

"I have bad news for all of you," he announced. "Our engineer has not returned. The truth is, I fear he drank too much blackberry juice and has fallen asleep under a hedge somewhere. Does anyone in this car know how to drive a train?"

And he glanced anxiously around him. Not a paw went up.

"Do you mean to say that we can't get out of here?" demanded the raccoon.

Then Anatole raised his hand. "I know something about trains. I believe I could drive it if the squirrel would help me."

"I suppose I had better come, too," said Plumpet, "in case a pair of stout claws is needed."

The squirrel was only too happy to help. He threw a shovel of coal on the fire. Anatole opened the throttle and Plumpet pulled the whistle cord. Slowly the train began to move through the enormous tree, out of the city.

"Do any other trains use this track?" asked Anatole.

"Nobody uses this track but us," said the squirrel.

"Good," said Anatole. And Plumpet curled up by the firebox for a nap.

As the train entered the woods, thunder exploded close by and lightning danced on the tracks. Plumpet woke up in alarm.

"There's the river ahead of us," shouted the squirrel, "but where's the bridge? Stop the train!"

Hastily Anatole closed the throttle.

"I thought the train crossed the river by boat," said Anatole. "But I don't see a boat. How did the fox do it?"

"I don't know," said the squirrel crossly. "I pay attention to my own job. How should I know what the fox did?"

The train chugged to a stop.

"Excuse me," said Anatole, standing up.

"I'm coming with you," said Plumpet.

Anatole walked through the cars until he found the two owls in bonnets. Of all the creatures on the train, they alone were wide awake.

"Ladies," he said, "I know it's very wet outside, but I need someone who can fly and who can see in the dark. Somewhere there's a boat that will take us across the river, and I can't find it."

The owls took their bonnets and folded them carefully on the seat.

"Open the window," chirped the big owl.

"Lend us a paw," said Plumpet. And she bit the Barbary sheep very gently on the neck and the raccoon very gently on the tail. They woke up at once.

"Together, now, push!" shouted Anatole.

The Barbary sheep and the raccoon and the cat and Anatole all pushed. The window flew open, and the rain rushed in, and the birds flew out.

"Close the window!" cackled the hen on the baggage rack.

"What's the matter?" asked a rabbit, rubbing his eyes.

"We're stuck," said Plumpet. "Nothing to worry about."

All over the car, animals woke and looked about them in bewilderment. Anatole pressed his nose to the window. Suddenly he saw two pale shapes fluttering outside.

"There they are! Push!"

The window flew up, and the owls flew in.

"Achoo," sneezed the small owl. "We saw a hundred white lions."

"God bless you," exclaimed the turtle. "Lions!"

"An old man was sitting with them," added the big owl.

"Somebody must go and ask him for help," said the raccoon.

"I'll go," said Anatole. "After all, I'm the engineer."

"We'll both go," announced Plumpet. "Open the door. In such weather I'm glad I do not wear clothes that wrinkle and muss."

The Barbary sheep and the turtle opened the door, and the boy and the cat stepped out.

Suddenly the rain stopped. Ahead of them, the river eddied white in the moonlight. On the bank lay the lions, their heads on their paws, and in their midst sat an old fisherman dressed in a sheepskin coat.

"He looks like a thistle," whispered Plumpet. "White hair, white beard, white coat, white boots. I think he fell into a flour barrel."

"Please, sir," called Anatole.

The lions rumbled and lifted their heads.

"Who are you?" roared the old man.

"I am Anatole. I am driving the train to the mainland, and I want to cross the river. Where's the boat?"

"This is my river, and my lions are the boat," said the old man. "What will you pay me for taking you across?"

"What do you want?" asked Anatole.

"The fox always gives me a piece of the sky."

Anatole shook his head. "But I don't have such a thing."

"Maybe you have a piece hidden in your pockets?" asked the old man.

Anatole turned his pockets inside out. "All I have is this watch."

The old man seized the watch. "How marvelous! A watch from the world where people still keep time!"

"It doesn't run," said Anatole. "Purely sentimental value. Please give it back."

The old man whistled a little tune. Then he said, "If you want me to carry your train across the river, give me the watch."

Silently Anatole handed him the watch.

Then the old man glanced down at Anatole's shoes. "How marvelous! Shoes from the world where things still wear out!"

"My sneakers? They're all raggedy," said Anatole nervously. "And the laces are broken."

The old man whistled a little tune. Then he said, "If you want me to carry your train across the river, give me your shoes."

So Anatole took off his shoes and gave them to the old man, who took off his white boots and put on the sneakers. Much to Anatole's surprise, they fitted him.

Then the old man glanced up at Anatole's shirt and

sighed. "What a wonderful shirt! What is that inscription on it?"

"My T-shirt? It says *Oxford, Michigan, Gravel Capital of the World.* I got it when I went to visit my grandma."

"Your grandma lives in a gravel pit?" inquired the old man.

"No," said Anatole. "She lives in Oxford. Most everyone around there works at the pit."

"How marvelous!" exclaimed the old man. "A shirt from the world where people still go to work every morning!"

"It's very dirty," said Anatole. "You should see the collar."

The old man whistled a little tune. Then he said, "If you want me to carry your train across the river, give me your shirt."

So Anatole took off his T-shirt and gave it to the old man, who took off his sheepskin coat and put on the shirt. Much to Anatole's surprise, it fitted him.

Then the old man said, "I've taken your clothes. You shall have mine. Now drive your train down to the river. I will command my lions to form a raft with their bodies. Drive your train over their backs. My lions are very strong. And I will stand at the front of the raft and pole you across."

The old man walked among his lions and called them down to the water. Anatole put on the old man's boots and coat.

"Very handsome," said Plumpet. "Let's go."

"SILENTLY ANATOLE HANDED HIM THE WATCH."

But Anatole could not move. His feet seemed glued to the earth.

"I can't," he said. "These clothes are too heavy."

"What a shame!" clucked Plumpet. "Isn't there some way of carrying them?"

Anatole kicked off the boots and pulled off the coat.

"It's no use. We'd better hurry. We're still a long way from home."

And he climbed aboard the train.

The hen on the baggage rack cocked her head at him.

"You've shed your clothes," she observed. "Are you moulting?"

"No," said Anatole. "Plumpet, tell everyone in the cars we're on our way."

The train rolled forward. Pressed close together, the lions formed a fine raft. At the head of them stood the old man, pushing the raft with a pole. And so smoothly did he dip the pole in and out that no one felt the train roll onto the opposite bank. When Anatole stuck his head out of the window, the lions looked like so many white boulders scattered in the river and the old man was nowhere to be seen. Ahead of them stretched a clearing—how different St. John's Meadow looked at night!

Then they came to a town, and then another town. One by one the animals got off.

Suddenly Anatole smelled something he loved, the apple trees and the mint in his mother's garden at home.

"Plumpet, wake up. This is our stop."

"Thank you for your help," said the squirrel, and he

jumped up on the engineer's seat. "We wouldn't have made it without you."

Anatole and Plumpet stood in the middle of the garden, in the middle of the night. The train was gone.

"You're a hero," said Plumpet.

"I don't feel like a hero. I'm sleepy," said Anatole.

"Go to bed then. I'm going out mousing for an hour or two. And I have promises to keep in the morning."

And that's why the next morning Anatole found himself looking out of his window at Plumpet, who was digging under the apple tree. With her claws she dug a little hole, and in the hole she planted the sprig of catnip she'd picked in St. John's Meadow. And as she planted, she sang lustily for anyone who cared to listen:

> "O, the racing of the sun
> and the rising of the moon.
> These flowers green and tall
> must go the way of all,
> and winter comes too soon.

> "O, the sparrows in the sky,
> and the dragons in the sea.
> In mad or merry weather,
> we'll take our rest together
> under the apple tree."

The Wise Soldier
of Sellebak

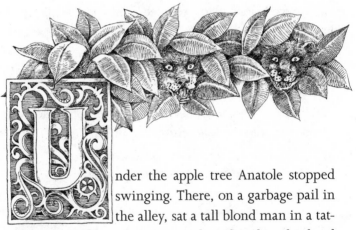

Under the apple tree Anatole stopped swinging. There, on a garbage pail in the alley, sat a tall blond man in a tattered blue uniform, eating an apple and cocking his head to hear Anatole's mother as she practiced "Awake, Ye Wintry Earth" in an uncertain alto for the Sunday service.

So of course Anatole walked right up to the garbage pail and waited for the man to speak.

But the stranger went right on eating his apple.

"Who are you?" demanded Anatole.

The stranger shook his head. "Don't know. Woke up this morning to find I'd been robbed of everything I had. Name, address, destination."

Anatole was so surprised that for a moment he could think of nothing to say. Still, he wanted to help.

"Did you check your pockets?" he inquired.

"What do you know about that!" The man slapped his knee. "Forgot to check my pockets."

He rummaged through his pockets and pulled out a large tooth.

"It once belonged to a reindeer," he said. "I carry it for luck."

As soon as he saw the tooth, Anatole wanted to trade his rabbit's foot for it, but the stranger was already tucking it carefully out of sight. Then he tried another pocket and found a tiny folder, cut like a canister, on which was printed in gold the following inscription:

> *Van Houten's Cocoa, on the tables of the world.*
> A Perfect Beverage
> combining Strength,
> Purity, and Solubility.
> *Open here.*

When he opened it, up popped a little paper table set for two: two painted plates, two cups of painted cocoa, two painted sugar buns.

"Very tasty," said the stranger. "Instant breakfast. Want some?"

"No thanks," said Anatole. "I've already eaten mine."

"Put it in your pocket then," said the stranger. "Pockets are a great invention. Did you know my mother was a kangaroo? Perhaps the earth is but a—" He waved his arms histrionically, searching for the word.

"A marble?" suggested Anatole.

"A marble, right! A marble in the pocket of God. When I was a kid, I used to pick pockets in reverse. Instead of taking things out, I put things in. A gumdrop here. A candy cane there. Now how did this ad for Van Houten's cocoa get in my pocket?"

"Maybe you're a traveling salesman," said Anatole.

But the stranger was rummaging through his pockets again. This time he pulled out a silver Maltese cross.

"Now what in the name of heaven is this?" he exclaimed.

"That's a war medal," said Anatole. "Oh, let me look at it. I'm very interested in war. There's writing on the back. E-R-I-K H-A-N-S-O-N."

"Erik Hanson!" shouted the stranger. "Why, I'm Erik Hanson of the 147th Regiment. That's two things I remember."

"Four," said Anatole. "Your mother is a kangaroo and you put things in people's pockets."

"I forgot to tell you—what is your name?"

"Anatole."

"Well, Anatole, I forgot to tell you I'm an awful liar and you can't believe half of what I say. But what army did I serve with, I wonder?"

"Wait right here," said Anatole.

He darted into his house, pulled all the galoshes out of the hall closet, and—wonder of wonders!—there lay his shoebox of lead soldiers, just where he remembered putting it away. Then he ran into the bathroom and grabbed a book that was lying on the radiator. At night in the bathtub he liked to read a chapter from *So You Want to Be a Magician*. And finally he raced back to Erik Hanson, half afraid he would find him gone.

But there he sat, swinging to and fro on Anatole's swing, dragging his feet in the dandelions. Anatole opened the box of soldiers to show him, and Erik peered in, very much interested.

"You have a fine collection. I had a wooden soldier when I was a kid. And if you opened him up, you found another one, only smaller. And if you opened him up, you found another one, still smaller. The smallest was no bigger than a flea's ear. I never saw it, but I knew it was there. Some things you have to take on faith. Well, Anatole, do you find anyone like me in that box?"

"Here's a soldier in a blue uniform rather like yours," said Anatole, picking one out. "Maybe you're an infantry corporal of the U.S. Army, 1864."

"That would make me awfully old," said Erik, laughing. "Over a hundred."

"How old are you?" asked Anatole.

"BUT THERE HE SAT, SWINGING TO AND FRO ON ANATOLE'S SWING,
DRAGGING HIS FEET IN THE DANDELIONS."

Erik shrugged. His rough pink skin wrinkled merrily around his eyes. His hair was so pale that you could not tell whether to call it blond or white. He might have been twenty; he might have been fifty.

"I brought out my magic book, too," said Anatole. "It tells how to find things like coins and playing cards. And it's full of nifty magic words. Abracadabra! Puziel, guziel, psdiel, zap!"

"See if there's a chapter on finding lost people," said Erik.

Anatole opened the book.

"Darn it, this isn't my book of magic. It's my book of games."

"Oh, I love games," exclaimed Erik. "What games does your book have?"

"Fox and Goose," read Anatole, flipping through the pages, "Bob-Cherry, Baste the Bear, May I, The Quickest Way of Going to Anywhere..."

"What is the quickest way?" asked Erik. "I don't know that game."

So Anatole read:

"Let the players write the name of London Town (or the desired destination) on a paper and cast it into the middle of the circle. Then, let them take hands and run around the circle very fast, chanting:

"'See saw sacradown,
which is the way to London Town?
(Insert desired destination.)

One foot up and the other foot down,
that is the way to London Town.
(One journey to a customer.)'"

"That sounds like a magic spell," said Erik. "Ahoy, boys, I'm off to Hawaii!"

"No, it's not a magic spell. It doesn't have any magic words."

"Nonsense," said Erik. "You know why those words don't sound magic? Because we know what they mean. Now if I were a one-eyed bull snake and heard those words, I'd figure they were the most magical things around. Let's write the name of my town on a piece of paper, and then let's draw a circle..."

"You don't remember the name of your town," Anatole reminded him.

"Quite true. I forgot. So let's write. 'Erik's home.'"

Anatole ran once more to the house and fetched paper and pencil from the kitchen table and wrote very carefully:

Erik's Home

Under the apple tree, Anatole drew a circle in the grass with his heel and cast down the paper.

"Now, let's take hands," said Erik, "and start running."

And as they ran, they shouted:

"See saw sacradown,
which is the way to Erik's home?

One foot up and the other foot down,
that is the way to Erik's home."

Almost immediately their feet left the ground and
sped effortlessly over the tops of the trees and then over
the clouds. Anatole found it amazing that his feet, so
long accustomed to the ground, could make a road of the
air. Through a break in the clouds, Anatole saw the Statue
of Liberty. And then he found himself running beside
Erik over the open sea.

Waves heaped themselves up and tumbled toward
them like mountains, on which the sun shone so bril-
liantly that you would have thought they were running
on silver.

"Look," called Erik, "a boat! Let's give them a scare,
shall we?"

An ocean liner was passing them, slowly and steadily,
and they ran alongside it so close that Anatole could see
men and women dancing in the main ballroom, and he
could hear the orchestra playing "Blue Moon." Through
a porthole he could look into the kitchen, where two
waiters were clinking glasses. The cozy smell of tobacco
and cabbage nearly made him cry.

At the back of the ship huddled several passengers in
blankets. A child's voice cried out, "I see a man and a boy
running on the sea!"

And the grownups all looked up at the broken clouds
of the evening sky, for of course that is the reasonable
place to find the unexpected shapes of things.

Night came swiftly and swallowed the ship, but a thin crack of light broke on the horizon ahead of them. Then the sun popped up like a luminous peach, silhouetting a fishing boat where three old men rowed toward a distant shore.

"Hey, fishermen," called Erik, "what country is that?"

"Norway," called back the fishermen, who had seen stranger sights in the sea than a man and a boy running on the water. They had not run very long before Anatole spied a ferryboat ahead of them, and as they drew near, they heard childish voices singing:

> "*Ja, vi elsker dette landet*
> Yes, we love this land of ours..."

There on the main deck stood a stout man in uniform, directing a chorus of school children.

"Hey, schoolmaster," called Erik, "what town is that?"

The schoolmaster was too astonished to answer, but the children cried out joyously, "Fredrikstad, Fredrikstad."

At these words, Anatole felt his feet turn abruptly. Now they carried him over a town of small wooden houses, past a brickyard, and then suddenly his feet stopped, and Anatole tumbled into a new-mown pasture, and Erik tumbled on top of him.

Anatole sat up.

"Erik, where are we?"

Erik's face looked as if the sun had just risen in it.

"In Sellebak. And you won't find it in the *World Atlas*, either. What nerve to call itself a *World Atlas* and not include Sellebak! Do you see that house at the edge of the pasture? I was born in that house. Do you see that tall man standing in the doorway? That's my father. He sailed all over the world when I was little. He's bald as a stone now; he wasn't then. And that small woman beside him, she's my mother. Her hands are tinier than yours, Anatole. I used to play with her gloves in church. Oh, Anatole, I remember, I remember!"

By nightfall, everyone in Sellebak knew that Erik Hanson had returned, bringing with him a boy who was rumored to be a great magician. Friends came all the way from Fredrikstad to see him. To make certain of a warm welcome, each one brought something to eat, until Fru Hanson's kitchen could hold no more baskets of cheese, no more platters of herring and onions and fish cakes, and no more jars of cloudberry jam. Herr Hanson set up a table outside, a safe distance from the gooseberry bushes that were just ripening and a great temptation to the children. Only Anatole noticed the old man who stood by the biggest bush eating gooseberries, as if he thought himself invisible or everyone else blind. He did not seem to belong to any of the visiting families.

Over a bowl of steaming cabbage, Erik remembered part of his story.

"You were eighteen and you enlisted," said his mother, "and I never saw you again. It was a beautiful sunny day in June, just like this one."

"I remember," said Erik. "And I remember growing up in this house. I remember the stove where I loved to warm myself. It had a picture of Vulcan on the door."

"I still have that stove," said his mother, wiping her glasses and blowing her nose.

"And I remember the winter that the hens froze on their perch," said Erik. "And I remember how I loved molasses on brown bread, and you told me how sugar and butter on white bread tasted much better, only there wasn't any."

"That was at the beginning of the war," said Herr Hanson. "Do you remember the peaches I used to send you from America? Tell me, Anatole, do you like peaches?"

"Yes, indeed," said Anatole, taking a second helping of fish cakes.

"Good," said Herr Hanson. "Shows you have good sense. Magic is fine, but I don't understand it. I think perhaps Erik is not quite right in his head; all these stories about running across the ocean. Well, well. We must believe in God and accept what happens."

A stout young woman with a crown of blond braids on her head and a child in her arms came shyly up to Erik.

"Do you remember me, Erik? You promised to marry me once. Well, that was a long time ago, and I married another man. But I still remember the song you sang to me."

And the whole company fell silent as she sang, slowly and clearly:

"How lovely is your golden hair,
blessed is he who can win you."

The sun danced in the leaves of the plum tree, and Fru Hanson wiped her glasses.

"That was thirty years ago," said Erik. "I remember all of you. I remember the day I went off to fight. But of that thirty years between that day and this, I remember nothing."

He stood up and walked around the yard, whispering, "Thirty years lost! Thirty years lost! What I wouldn't give to see them again!"

And Anatole, stumbling after him, bumped smack into the old man who was still helping himself to the ripe gooseberries.

"Excuse me," said Anatole.

"So you wish to turn back the sun," called the old man to Erik. "Then it's to the sun you must go, my lad. My great-grandfather journeyed there once."

"Is it possible?" exclaimed Erik.

"Not for you," said the old man, laughing. "The sun speaks only to children. If anyone can find the sun's house, it's this boy here. But the way is long and very difficult."

"Very difficult?" asked Anatole, who loved a good adventure if it was not too dangerous.

"Of course," said the old man, "but there are always people who want to make the journey because there are always people who want to be magicians."

"Can the sun make me into a magician?"

The old man shook his head. "The sun won't, but the journey will. It's the journeys we make for others that give us the power to change ourselves. The hardest part is getting home again, for you can't go home the way you left it. Nobody can give you the magic to take you home. You have to find that magic on your own."

"Oh, Anatole," exclaimed Erik, "say you'll go."

"Of course you can always be an ordinary magician who pulls rabbits out of hats and doves out of handkerchiefs," said the old man.

"No," said Anatole, "I want to be a real magician. How do I find the house of the sun?"

The old man looked very pleased. "I will give you some runes to say."

"Runes?" asked Anatole, puzzled. "What are runes?"

The old man smiled. "Runes are the magic words of the old gods who lived here before the Christians came."

"I love magic words," said Anatole.

"Yes, I could tell that at a glance. And so these words will probably disappoint you. They are perfectly clear, and yet they make no sense. They are important, yet they teach you nothing. Do you see that hill just beyond the pasture, across the road?"

"I see it. Erik and I landed near there."

"If you stand on that hill and say the runes aloud, one of the four winds will come to help you. I don't know which one. A fair wind is a great help in reaching the house of the sun. If you are in trouble, say the runes backward. But you can only use the runes in this way once."

"Thirty years! I shall have my thirty years again!" crowed Erik.

"Tell me the runes," begged Anatole.

The old man put his mouth close to Anatole's ear so that Erik shouldn't hear him.

> "9 were Nothe's sisters:
> Then the 9 was 8
> and the 8 was 7
> and the 7 was 6
> and the 6 was 5
> and the 5 was 4
> and the 4 was 3
> and the 3 was 2
> and the 2 was 1
> and the 1 was none."

"Who are Nothe's sisters?" asked Anatole.

"They are the nine stars who bring in the night. They're bringing it in now, though we can't see it coming yet. Better hurry, for if the night catches you, you'll never find your way home."

"Good-bye, Erik," said Anatole, beginning to feel a little anxious.

And to his amazement, Erik lifted him off the ground and kissed him.

"If I can help you, Anatole, call me. If you need a war fought or a field plowed—"

"I'll come straight to you," Anatole promised.

And he set off with great strides across the pasture for fear the smell of Fru Hanson's savory pancakes would make him turn back.

The hill looked at him the way any hill at home would look at him; it said, *Climb me.* Anatole started to climb, stepping carefully in his sneakers over the slabs of stone that broke like wrinkled faces through the grass. When he reached the top, he saw he was standing where four pastures met. To the east and the south, he saw clusters of white houses dreaming on the horizon, with an uncertain road glinting between them. To the west sparkled a church as white and small as a tooth. To the north rose another hill.

Anatole stood on a rock and said gravely:

"9 were Nothe's sisters:
Then the 9 was 8
and the 8 was 7
and the 7 was 6
and the 6 was 5
and the 5 was 4
and the 4 was 3
and the 3 was 2
and the 2 was 1
and the 1 was none."

Nothing happened.

A flock of gulls fluttered down like handkerchiefs into the pasture. Then all at once Anatole spied a tiny speck in

the sky that, as it flew nearer, took the shape first of a
bird and then of an angel. But what, thought Anatole,
could it be?

It was a man in a suit as white as snow and as bright
as water, and he was riding a book, and when he saw
Anatole, he sang out, "Who called the West Wind?"

"Me," said Anatole, abashed at this strange figure. "I
want to go to the house of the sun."

"And what will you do when you find it?" asked the
West Wind.

"I'll ask the sun to give Erik Hanson his thirty lost
years and to send me home again, for I can't go home the
way I came."

The West Wind opened his book, which was the sad
color of twilight, and turned the pages one by one. They
gave off a most pleasant perfume, which Anatole saw
came not from the paper but from the letters printed
there. A castle and vineyard glowed in a sunlit D; the
harvesters were carrying baskets of grapes on their heads,
and Anatole could hear the women singing, though he
could not understand the words. A formal garden grew
in a shady O; the gardener tying back the delphiniums
glanced up at Anatole and tipped his hat.

When the West Wind had turned every page, he closed
the book, and the music stopped abruptly and the fragrance of the flowers disappeared.

"The house of the sun," he said thoughtfully. "To tell
you the truth, I don't know the way, but I'll take you to

"IT WAS A MAN IN A SUIT AS WHITE AS SNOW AND AS BRIGHT AS WATER,
AND HE WAS RIDING A BOOK..."

my brother the North Wind, who is stronger than I and flies farther."

Together they flew north, over pine forests and over the camps of the Lapps following the reindeer and over the ice fields to the top of the world, and alit on the roof of the biggest palace Anatole had ever seen. A hundred turrets, he figured, and two hundred flags stiff as postcards; five hundred diamond windows at least, chimneys thick as a forest, and everything cut from blue ice.

"The door is always frozen shut," said the West Wind. "We must fly down the great chimney."

"What is the great chimney?" asked Anatole.

"Wait and see."

Down the chimney they flew and crawled out of an ice fireplace into an enormous room. It had no furniture at all, nothing but a giant tree growing out of the floor to the ceiling. Perched on the lowest branch slept an eagle.

"Brother, wake up," urged the West Wind. "This boy wants to find the house of the sun. Farewell!"

And the West Wind flew back up the chimney.

The North Wind opened his eyes. "You will find the house of the sun at the top of this tree."

"How far is it to the top?" asked Anatole, who loved to climb trees.

"I do not know. But halfway up takes a hundred years. Are you a hero of the golden age?"

"I don't think so," said Anatole.

"Well, it's worth finding out. Climb till you come to a

golden city nestled in the branches of the tree. It belongs to the sun's own finches, which sing to him day and night. Knock at the gate and ask for the magic drum that will carry you to the house of the sun. And if they give you the drum, sit on it and say, 'Drum, drum, fly to the sun,' and it will take you there directly. Only do not be afraid of anything you meet on the way."

"Thank you," said Anatole.

The trunk of the tree grew thick as a wall. Anatole could not even see where it curved around to the other side. He looked up into the branches. No light broke through at the top. The tree grew into a great darkness.

"It's best not to think about the top," said the North Wind. "It's best just to start climbing."

So Anatole put his foot on the first low branch and sprang up into the tree.

At first he found the climbing fun. He met nobody on the way except two squirrels who chattered to him, "What news?" Anatole smiled and shook his head. And then, as he had no one else to talk to, he talked to himself.

"It's just like climbing the big pine tree in Grandma and Grandpa's yard. When I was real little, it seemed like I'd never get to the top. Now I can shimmy up there easy, and I can look down and see Mr. Pederson across the street, mowing the lawn."

Though he squinted, he could see nothing beyond the branches that surrounded him. They seemed to stretch out forever, and the discovery made him feel lonely and a little scared.

"Oh, but I'm not alone. Lots of things live in trees. All kinds of birds make nests in trees—"

He broke off. He did not like to think of all the things that might live in this one. He wanted, very badly, a peanut butter and jelly sandwich and a nice saggy sofa to lie down on, like the one at home. He sank so deeply into this thought that he nearly forgot to hold onto the branch. That frightened him; he stopped, trembling, and sat down to rest. And in the silence of his resting he heard a thin cold sound.

"*Hsssss! Hsssss!*"

Quickly he glanced up. No wind blew, but the leaves shook. Behind them white blossoms nodded to him. Blossoms or—he drew his hand back in alarm. What he had taken for blossoms was a tangle of snakes, smiling and darting their tongues at him. And now that he was afraid, they drew closer to him, whispering, "*Hsssssss. Hsssss. Just you wait. Just you wait.*"

He jumped up and climbed away from them, but the branches sprang back as fast as he pushed them aside. When he could not move forward or backward, he sat down again, wondering what to do. The branches locked him into the darkness. He listened for the snakes. He did not hear them, but something else waited behind the leaves and saw his fear and growled softly.

The wind rocked the branch he was sitting on, and he

held it tightly, for he saw just behind the leaves, and very close to him, the faces of hideous dogs. Their eyes glowed like candles, and it seemed to Anatole that the whole tree was burning. Far off he heard the yelping of foxes and the cries of hunters.

With all his might, Anatole pushed himself through the thicket, closing his eyes so that he wouldn't have to look at the dogs. And who knows where he might have ended up if he hadn't bumped against a golden gate, set in a smooth golden wall that shone like a crown.

A goldfinch wearing a silver ruff opened the gate.

"Excuse me," said Anatole hastily, for the goldfinch immediately tried to shut it again, "have you the drum that flies to the sun?"

"Are you the one that's to have it?" asked the goldfinch.

"Yes," said Anatole.

"Who sent you?"

"The North Wind."

"Very well, I'll fetch it," said the goldfinch. "You may wait in my sentry box if you like. I've a bottle of dandelion wine on my desk. Help yourself. Have one for the road."

Before he could do so, the goldfinch returned bearing the drum in its claws.

"Don't jump off the drum till you reach the house of the sun. The moment you leave it, it will return to us."

"I'll be most careful," said Anatole.

He climbed on the drum and said, "Drum, drum, fly to the sun."

Immediately the drum swooped up and out of the tree, broke through the sky, and landed on a long white road in a broad, bare country. The road toward which the drum carried him ended at the door of a most peculiar house. It shone clear as glass and looked exactly like a pumpkin that has grown from a sunbeam. As the drum bumped along the road, an old woman appeared in the doorway.

"Well, well," said the old woman, "what have we here?"

Anatole jumped off the drum and whoosh! it vanished.

"I'm looking for the sun," said Anatole.

"Well, well," said the old woman, "I happen to be his mother. What do you want with him?"

"I want him to give Erik Hanson his thirty lost years and to send me home again, for I don't know the way and I can't go home the way I came."

"And what will you give me if I take you to see him?"

Anatole plunged his hands into his pockets. Nothing, nothing. No, wait, what was this? He pulled out the little advertisement for Van Houten's cocoa.

"A little book, is it?" inquired the old woman. "What's it called?"

"Van Houten's Cocoa," Anatole read bravely. "A Perfect Beverage combining Strength, Purity, and Solubility. Open here." He wanted to weep.

"It's magic, of course," said the old woman. "Otherwise you wouldn't have brought it. You would have brought me a cartload of pearls drawn by unicorns or a bushel of singing rubies. Such toys I see every day. But rarely does anyone bring me a magic book called *Van Houten's Cocoa*. What does it do?"

Anatole shook his head.

"Come, come. Does it turn rain into tigers? Princes into cabbages?"

"No," said Anatole.

And then he remembered the runes. So he put the little folder to his lips and over it he whispered:

"and the none was 1
and the 1 was 2
and the 2 was 3
and the 3 was 4
and the 4 was 5
and the 5 was 6
and the 6 was 7
and the 7 was 8
and the 8 was 9;
9 were Nothe's sisters."

"It's all or nothing," he added, and he opened the folder.

But instead of a tiny paper table set for two, there sprang forth a huge table set for forty. And such a setting! Wands of cowslip bread, platters of candied violets and marzipan marigolds, great tureens of daffodil soup and crocks of rose-petal jam. And in the middle, of course, stood a silver urn of cocoa from which flew a little pennant: *Van Houten's. On the table of the sun.*

"Oh, that's killing," cried the old woman, "perfectly killing! It's the best toy anyone has ever given me. Let me try it."

She shut the folder and the banquet disappeared.

She opened it and the banquet returned. The bread was still warm. Anatole had never smelled anything so delicious.

"Well, well," said the old woman, seizing a loaf and biting into it, "help yourself."

"Thank you," said Anatole. He ate two loaves of bread and three plates of violets, and then he laughed. What if his mother, who was always saying, "Eat, eat," could see him now! He felt so much better that he began to believe things would go well for him after all.

"What about the sun?" he inquired.

"Ah," said the old woman, "he's shining over Asia. Would you like to watch him?"

She led Anatole into the round glass house. In the middle gleamed a pool of water, and in that still water he saw the sun, but how different the sun looked in this mirror than in the skies at home. No moving ball of fire but an old man the color of embers, wearing a raven on each shoulder, and with each step he took, he grew older still.

"He'll be half dead when he arrives," said the old

woman, "and that is the time to catch him, for that's when he's the wisest. You must meet him on the road, for when he passes through the doorway of this house, he will turn into a little child, and then there's no seriousness in him at all, and he won't help you a bit."

So Anatole, sipping his cocoa, watched for the old man on the road. But the old woman saw farther than Anatole.

"That's he," she said. "Run to him quickly before he reaches the door."

Anatole bounded out of the house and down the road till he met the sun, who was creeping along, white-haired, squint-eyed, and more wrinkled than the sea. "Grack! Grack!" clucked the ravens on his shoulders.

"Sun!" called Anatole.

The sun peered all around him.

"Where are you?" he croaked. "I don't see well now, and my hearing is bad."

"I've come to ask you about Erik Hanson."

"Erik Hanson of Sellebak?" said the sun. "What about him?"

"He's lost thirty years of his life, and he wants them back."

"Well, he can't have them," said the sun crossly. "I won't give him time, but I will give him knowledge. He shall know everything that happened to him during those years. Will that do?"

"I guess it will have to do," said Anatole.

"I will send him my servants, Thought and Memory, my two trusty ravens who tell me all that goes on in the great world. They will show him his past. They'll show him how to turn hurts into blessings and dragons into princesses. And if he listens to them, he will be the greatest storyteller in Norway."

"He's a good storyteller right now," said Anatole, remembering how Erik once described his mother as a kangaroo.

"But if he does not want this knowledge," continued the sun, "he should send my servants away. Sometimes people forget what it causes them pain to remember. It is not easy for a soldier to remember the faces of the people he has killed."

They had arrived at the door, and no sooner had the sun passed through it than zzzzzz! the old man vanished and there stood a child, scarcely a year old, babbling and laughing and tumbling on the floor.

The old woman dipped the corner of her apron in the pool and scrubbed the child's face, and snatching a loaf of bread from the table, she pushed it into his hand.

"And now, outside with you. You must go and wake the children in Brazil."

"Wait!" cried Anatole. "You must tell me how to get home again."

But the sun ran laughing out the door.

"That's a pity," said the old woman, shaking her head. "Now you'll have to wander the earth until you find

"THE OLD WOMAN DIPPED THE CORNER OF HER APRON IN THE POOL
AND SCRUBBED THE CHILD'S FACE..."

your road, for the sun talks to a man only once in his life, and you've had your chance."

Anatole burst into tears. But suddenly he felt a flutter of wings brush his cheek, and there on his shoulder sat the sun's raven.

"I am Thought," cawed the raven, "and I offer you my services. You cannot return home the way you came, by drum, by tree, or by wind, for the connections are uncertain and none of them runs on time. But I am swifter than the drum and the wind, and I am not rooted in any one place like the tree."

"What must I do?" asked Anatole.

"Think of your home. A real magician isn't afraid of what he doesn't understand. You are a real magician now."

So Anatole thought of his house and his swing and his mother singing "Awake, Ye Wintry Earth," and how she would soon go to the kitchen and start supper, meat loaf, maybe, and he thought how his papa would come home with a newspaper for himself and a gingerbread man for Anatole from the bakery, and he thought how no place was nicer than this place where two people loved him.

And he found himself sitting on his swing at twilight.

But this is not the end of the story. Two days before Christmas, early in the morning, Anatole saw a large black bird drop something on the windowsill outside his room. He opened the window and found a reindeer's tooth, which he recognized, and a book, which he did not. On the cover he read Erik Hanson's Saga. And inscribed on the flyleaf was the following message:

How can I ever thank you, dear Anatole? Here are the stories that Memory has told me and Thought has helped me to set down. The book is full of magic words, and they'll bring you many adventures if you take the trouble to learn what they mean.

Love, Erik

"HIGH IN THE TREES OVERHEAD HE HEARD A THIN SINGING..."

Sailing to Cythera

randmother never threw anything
away. If you left a seashell under the
piano at Christmas, you knew it would
still be there when you went to visit in June. Whenever
Anatole complained that he couldn't find his sneakers or
his dump truck, Grandma said, "You wouldn't believe
the stuff I've lost in this house. But everything turns up
in the wash. You go and play."

So he did. First he sewed on her sewing machine.

Then he wound her five clocks: a grandfather clock, a cuckoo clock, a clock set in the bosom of a brass stork, an alarm clock, and a porcelain clock with a ring of parrots dancing on its face under a glass dome. No two clocks kept exactly the same time, which was fine, said Grandma, because no two people do either.

Then he asked her if he could play kingdom and use her gold filigree candy dish for a crown.

"That's been lost for months," said Grandma.

Then he asked if he could play with her two silver birds that held salt and pepper.

"When they turn up," said Grandma.

Then he drummed on the piano, for it is very difficult to lose a piano. He played "The Frog He Would A-Wooing Go" with his big toe for Pizzicato, Grandma's black cat, who did not like children and who slept all day in front of the fireplace. Grandma always kept a fire burning, even in summer.

"Nothing is cozier than a fire," said Grandma, who did not have to chop wood for her fires but only to light the little jet over the grate and turn the gold key on the hearth and behold! out leaped two magnificent flames. Anatole called it magic. Grandma called it "natural gas."

"There are only two things you mustn't do," said Grandma. "Don't try to light the fireplace by yourself. Your mother singed her eyebrows off doing that when she was your age. And don't write on the wallpaper. It's very old. It came with the house."

"Can I touch the wallpaper?" asked Anatole.

Grandmother laughed.

"Of course you can! I touch it all the time. I can't really enjoy a thing unless I can touch it, can you?"

The wallpaper, which covered all the rooms in the house, showed a river dotted with islands where shepherds and shepherdesses danced and rowed about in small boats garlanded with roses. The shepherds, in blue coats and russet breeches, leaned pensively on golden crooks. The shepherdesses nodded like peonies ruffled by the wind and smiled under their broad straw hats. Some wore masks and some wore fantastic wigs hung with small trumpets and shells.

And far beyond them, so faint you could scarcely make it out, glittered a bridge and the towers of a city.

And when you had seen all this, you saw it again, for the pattern repeated itself over and over again, except for the bridge and the city, which only occurred over the umbrella stand in the front hall.

"Who are those people?" asked Anatole, sitting beside his grandmother on the stairs.

"This woman I call Madame d'Aulnoy," said Grandma, pointing to a buxom woman in enormous pink skirts and a satin stomacher. "You can see she's sensible; she's not wearing a wig. And this girl in the rowboat is her daughter, Thérèse. And here's where I spilled the chicken soup I was carrying up to Grandpa when he was sick. It's the very shape of a dragon."

And suddenly she started to sing:

> "On the bridge of Avignon
> they are dancing, they are dancing,
> On the bridge of Avignon
> they are dancing, every one."

"I like that song," said Anatole.

"That's all I remember learning in fourth grade," said Grandma. "That and 'Frère Jacques.' I must have learned more, but the rest escapes me."

Every warm evening after supper, Grandma helped Grandpa into the big wicker chair on the back porch and surrounded him with pillows. Anatole brought him the newspaper, and then he and Grandma sat together on the swing, cool in the shadow of the honeysuckle bush that pressed against the screen. Nobody said much. Anatole chewed a cinnamon-stick cigar. Then Grandma, incited by the smell of cinnamon, fetched ginger ale for Grandpa and Anatole and fixed a cup of Sanka for herself because she'd lost the canister of tea. And when she picked up the empty glasses, she tested the left arm of Grandpa's chair, which wobbled.

"Jon will fix it. He can fix anything. A man like that is one in a million."

"Where does Jon go every evening?" asked Anatole one day.

"Down to the Schiller Inn for a mug of beer."

"Don't we have any beer?" asked Anatole.

"No," said Grandma. "I don't like it at all, except for the foam on top. That's the part I like. Don't let me forget about that armrest."

And they would all forget until the next evening.

Jon lived in the spare room and helped take care of Grandpa, who was twenty years older than Grandma and had forgotten how to walk. Sometimes he could not remember Anatole's name, but he always remembered to smile at him. Sometimes he said peculiar things like "Isn't it time to light the lamps?" or "Isn't it time to meet the boat?"

Then Grandma would kiss him and say, "Did you ever hear such nonsense? Grandpa, who do you love?"

"You," said Grandpa, taking Grandma's hand.

And then they heard the front door slam, and Grandma would say, "Jon's home. It's eight o'clock. Time for you to go to bed."

What Anatole minded about going to bed was the dark space under the bed. The bed stood in the room where his mother had slept as a child, and his mother's dolls still sat on the high shelves over the chest of drawers. Their china heads gleamed and their glass eyes followed him about. The ceiling had stars pasted on it, and the stars glowed in the dark. He would have preferred another room, but Grandma always put him in this one, and he didn't want to admit he was afraid.

He had found a way of climbing into bed that helped

a little. If he sprang from the door straight across the floor, he reached the bed in a single bound, so that the dark space under the bed hardly even saw him coming.

Then he waited until Grandma came in and sang to him, for when the sun lazed in the trees outside, Anatole had trouble falling asleep, and on the longest day of the year, which Grandmother called "Midsummer's Eve," he couldn't sleep at all, although she'd let him stay up an hour later than usual.

On that night he lay wrapped in his bathrobe, wide awake, waiting. Nobody came. He heard Jon's footsteps in the hall, and he called out, "Where's Grandma?"

Jon stuck his head through the door. "You still awake?"

Anatole nodded.

"You want a glass of water?"

"I want Grandma to come and sing to me."

"She can't," said Jon. "Have a toothpick."

"Why not?" asked Anatole, sticking the toothpick into his mouth.

"She's watching Lawrence Welk. The band is playing 'Let Me Call You Sweetheart,' and that's her favorite. Tell you what. I'll sing to you." He sat down on the bed. "What does she sing?"

"'On the Bridge of Avignon.'"

"Don't know that one," said Jon.

"'Nearer My God to Thee.'"

"Tell you what," said Jon, sitting down in the rocker.

"Let me sing you one I picked up while I was herding sheep in Nevada."

"Is it about sheep?"

And Jon sang, in a scratchy voice that sounded as if he'd kept it closed up in a pickle bottle for years:

> "What'll we do with a drunken sailor,
> What'll we do with a drunken sailor,
> What'll we do with a drunken sailor,
> Early in the morning?
>
> "Pull out the plug and wet him all over,
> Pull out the plug and wet him all over,
> Pull out the plug and wet him all over,
> Early in the morning."

And when Anatole looked at the wallpaper over his bed, he thought he saw, far away, a one-masted schooner and the drunken sailor, quite drenched, sleeping on a pile of rigging.

Outside the window, the sun dropped slowly behind roofs and chimneys and the feathery tops of trees. But a bright stillness quickened everything in the room, and Jon, who hated to end the song, turned it into a new one.

> "The water is wide,
> I cannot cross it,
> and neither have I wings to fly—"

He yawned hugely and sang the last stanzas with his
eyes shut.

> "Give me a boat that can carry two,
> and both shall row, my true love and I."

And Anatole could see the True Love in her little rowboat, fluttering her handkerchief at him, and now her
boat bumped against Jon's shoulder, but he sat as quiet as
a mountain, for he had fallen asleep, silhouetted against
a light that was breaking over the water, brighter and
brighter. The sun was rising in the country of the wallpaper.

The True Love, in a green tunic with flowers in her
hair, motioned Anatole toward the boat.

"Hurry, or we'll miss the fair, and the boat to Cythera
will leave without us!"

Anatole got in and sat down. He was too bewildered
to ask, "What fair?" and "Where is Cythera?" How queer
it felt to drift behind the chest of drawers! He saw that
Grandma's French dictionary had fallen behind it and lay
covered with dust. The dolls looked longingly after him,
like friends waving him off on a long journey.

"Your costume is lovely," said the True Love. "Did you
get it at Auberge's?"

Anatole looked down at his bathrobe.

"My grandmother gave it to me."

"And who's your grandmother?" asked the True Love.
And though he knew she had another name besides

"THE DOLLS LOOKED LONGINGLY AFTER HIM, LIKE FRIENDS WAVING HIM
OFF ON A LONG JOURNEY."

"Grandmother," he could not remember it for the life of him. "She lives back there, over the water," he answered, trying to sound casual. "Are you Madame d'Aulnoy?"

The True Love burst out laughing.

"I beg your pardon, Madame d'Aulnoy is my mother. If you will not tell me your grandmother's name, perhaps you will tell me yours."

But to his alarm, Anatole found that he could not remember his own name, either! The comfortable furniture of his room was rapidly vanishing, like a skyline of untenanted buildings. The True Love dipped her oars in and out, and water lilies sank away under the boat and popped up on the other side. The air smelled deliciously of flowers and cinnamon. Suddenly he remembered a name. It was not his own, but he said it anyway.

"Frère Jacques."

The True Love clapped her hands.

"Oh, you're a monk, of course. I should have guessed. Now you must ask me who I am."

"Are you Thérèse?"

"No, no, you must look at my costume. Can't you tell who I am?"

Anatole stared at her sandals and the bow and quiverful of arrows resting on her shoulder. She was very pretty, and she was chewing a blond spit curl that had escaped her crown of violets.

"No, I can't guess," he said at last.

"It is not polite to say *no*. You must say, 'I beg your pardon.'"

"I beg your pardon," said Anatole.

"I forgive you. I am Diana of the Hunt today, so I must forgive everyone who asks me. Do you think I am beautiful?"

"Yes," said Anatole, suddenly embarrassed.

"Thank you. You may call me Thérèse if you like."

The boat was gliding over the pebbly nests of half a dozen fish. Frogs sat like pulsing emeralds under the elderberry bushes on the banks. Suddenly a flock of orioles flashed overhead, and Anatole heard a burst of trumpets.

"Look," cried Thérèse, "on the bridge, everyone is dancing! Here, take an oar."

Pulling his oar hard as they rounded the bend, he saw over his shoulder hundreds of boats moored along the shore and just beyond them the bridge with its broad arches standing in the water and its delicate crown of booths and flags sparkling on top. And on the other side of the bridge he saw a ship, carved like a huge scallop, garlanded with roses. A thin sail fluttered from the single mast.

"Whose boat is that?" asked Anatole.

"That boat belongs to the Emperor of the Moon. That's the boat to Cythera."

"And where is Cythera?" asked Anatole.

But Thérèse seemed not to hear.

The boat nosed gently into the reeds. Thérèse jumped out, and Anatole tied it to a large honeysuckle bush. Shepherds and shepherdesses were hurrying up the grassy hill to the fair.

"And now you must take my arm," said Thérèse.

As they crested the hill, the fair blossomed before them. Stalls and shops packed the narrow street. The air glittered with handkerchiefs and silks, sausages and sea-shells, feathers and flowers, butterflies and candlesticks and tambourines. An old woman dozed behind a moun-tain of melons.

"Life, life!" shouted the wine merchant, pushing through the crowd with a casket of brandy on his back.

"Knives sharpened!"

"Mend your bellows, mister?"

"Teeth pulled here!"

"Here's health," cried the watercress woman, "two francs a bunch!"

Anatole ducked to avoid a girl carrying a tray of milk pots on her head.

"Ah, there's a puppet show," said Thérèse. "Let's go watch. And look as if you think I am very beautiful."

"But I do think so," protested Anatole.

Thérèse stamped her foot.

"What good is that to me if the others don't see it?"

They jostled themselves a place close to the front. A man dressed in rags and bells was packing away the pup-pets, but the curtain rose on a tableau of trained dogs, who sat at a table and ate with knives and forks. Anatole clapped hard. Thérèse was not watching. She kept glanc-ing at a clown in a white suit who shambled over to them, his mandolin under his arm.

"Hello, Gilles," Thérèse greeted him, curling her lip as if she didn't like him a bit. "This is my friend, Frère Jacques."

Anatole smiled and felt someone lay an arm around his shoulder and draw him aside. He turned and met the eyes of a red-faced fellow dressed all in stripes like peppermint candy, who whispered into his ear, "May I introduce myself? Mezzetin is the name, sir, friend of Gilles and the lady Thérèse. And now may I warn you to leave Mademoiselle Thérèse as soon as possible?"

"But why?" asked Anatole.

"Because she is determined to take the ship to Cythera, sir, a trip as dangerous as it is foolish. The Blimlim raised a storm last night, and three ships sank in the waters off Cythera."

"What," said Anatole, "is the Blimlim?"

Mezzetin lowered his voice still more, so that Anatole could scarcely hear him.

"The Blimlim is a monster who lives on the island. No one has seen him, sir, but you may read about him in the old histories. He has the body of a lizard, the head of an eagle, the wings of an albatross, and he's as big as a house—"

"Wait," interrupted Anatole. "If no one has seen him, how do you know he's there?"

"Surely you know that you don't have to see someone to know he's there," whispered Mezzetin.

Anatole thought of the dark space under his bed.

"Then why does anyone go to Cythera?" he asked, drawing back a little, for Mezzetin smelled strongly of garlic.

"Because the emperor has offered half his kingdom to the person who will bring him the skin of the Blimlim. And the island itself is a paradise, sir. No one grows old there. A race of children, winged like birds, lives in the air over the island, and they fill it with the most marvelous singing. The pebbles are pearls. The mermaids—"

He was drowned out by applause for a woman dancing with a sword in her mouth. A one-legged soldier sidled up to Anatole and held out a scimitar.

"Alms, kind sir. Do you want to buy this sword? I slew a dozen Turks with it."

"I don't think much of that," said Gilles. "It's easy to hurt somebody. It's very hard to love them." And he rolled his eyes sadly at Thérèse.

"Isn't it time to meet the boat?" said Thérèse. "Come, Frère Jacques. I know you aren't afraid."

"I should prefer to grow old than to be eaten by a Blimlim," snapped Mezzetin. "Good-bye."

"I'm going with Thérèse," said Gilles.

The three of them hurried into the crowd that was gathering on the shore. A man in a suit of pearls crossed the little gangplank and led the way into the ship.

"He's the Emperor of the Moon," said Thérèse with a sigh. "Isn't he splendid?"

Thousands of white handkerchiefs fluttered from the top of the bridge. As the ship sailed slowly down the river, a shepherd stopped strumming his mandolin under the willow trees and threw his cap in the air. His sheep, nibbling at the roses that festooned a ruined pavilion, lifted their heads in surprise. Then the cheering faded, the mist of distance blurred the bridge, and the ship entered the open sea.

The passengers paraded up and down the deck, laughing and chattering. At the back of the ship, the drunken sailor lay snoring on the coil of ropes. Anatole knew him at once and sat down beside him. A party of dancers dressed as apes strolled by them. Perhaps they really are apes, thought Anatole. But no, that white cat curled at the feet of the drunken sailor would not be washing itself so lazily.

"Hello, cat," said Anatole. "I have a cat like you at home." The cat stopped washing, its paw poised in the air.

"I am sure your cat is not at all like me, for I belong to Madame d'Aulnoy, and I speak nine languages."

"Is Madame d'Aulnoy on board?"

"She's right over there," answered the cat, "watching us."

And seeing that they had noticed her, a large woman with sharp features and kind eyes stepped away from the railing and held out her hands to Anatole.

"You are a stranger," she said. "Have you come to conquer the Blimlim?"

"No—I mean, I beg your pardon," stammered Anatole.

Madame d'Aulnoy stooped down and held his face in

her hands. Rings blazed on her fingers, and her dress, woven all of peacock feathers, dazzled his eyes.

"I'm not laughing at you," she said gravely. "I believe no one but a child can conquer the Blimlim. The emperor's soldiers won't try, not even for half the kingdom. 'We can't fight a mystery,' the captain said to me the other day. 'We have to know what weapons to use, guns or swords or traps.' I will tell you a secret," she whispered into his ear. "The real prize of the island is the golden bough. I would give anything just to see it, and the garden where it grows."

"Land ahoy!" shouted the drunken sailor in his sleep.

The cat jumped up on Anatole's shoulder. Everyone rushed to the front of the boat, and Anatole caught sight of Gilles and Thérèse.

"Frère Jacques," she called, "where have you been? Let's watch for mermaids. Mamma says the weather is just right."

Ahead of them shimmered the island, as green as the first leaves of spring misting over bare trees. Half a dozen horses trotting along the beach ran off into the woods. The boat seemed to be entering a golden twilight that was not of the world it had come from.

"How close night is to morning," said Gilles with a sigh.

"Does it ever get dark here?" Anatole asked the cat.

"Of course. We could put up lanterns as we do on the mainland. But because of the Blimlim we generally leave."

"I'd like to ride those horses we saw."

"They're wild," said the cat. "They live in the garden of the golden bough. I should advise you to leave them alone. Good-bye." And it sprang into the arms of Madame d'Aulnoy.

The boat hushed against the sand. One by one, as if entering a dance, the passengers climbed ashore. Anatole felt Madame d'Aulnoy touch his shoulder.

"Come, little Frère Jacques. You can join our party by the fountain of Venus."

"Please," said Anatole, "I want to go exploring."

Madame d'Aulnoy nodded.

"The other side of the island is wild, and if I were your mother, I should advise you not to go there. As I am not your mother, let me tell you only that it is very dangerous and very beautiful, and we sail for the mainland at sunset."

The moment she turned to leave, Anatole sprinted past the fountain into the forest beyond it. How glorious everything smelled! Violets and columbine sprang over the rocks, water trickled under the roots at his feet, and farther off the laughter of his friends by the fountain seemed to follow him.

"I'd like to find that garden," said Anatole to himself.

The words were hardly out of his mouth when a white horse stepped into his path and knelt down in front of him. Anatole jumped on its back at once, for he remembered that the horses lived in the garden. Now the quest seemed so simple to him that he wondered why nobody else had tried it. High in the trees overhead he heard a thin singing that sounded more seashell than human.

"That must be the flying children Mezzetin spoke of," he decided, but though he looked carefully and listened hard, he could neither see them nor make out the words of their song.

Directly ahead of him the trees grew much bigger and stood so close together that the horse could pass through them only with difficulty, as if it were entering a fortress. The air turned colder, and a deep silence dropped over everything.

"Horse," he said softly, "are you very close to—"

But he never finished, for something tremendous crashed through the trees behind them. The horse reared up, and Anatole tumbled into a bramble thicket.

"Horse, wait for me!" he called.

The horse was gone. Anatole could not even hear its hoofbeats. He scrambled to his feet and there, waiting to be noticed, crouched the Blimlim. Its green body glittered like a splendid coat of mail, its eyes flickered like bonfires, and its wings eclipsed the land of the light. It had claws like a lion and whiskers like a catfish, and it wore a gold filigree crown on its head.

"Don't run off," hissed the Blimlim. "Stay, and I'll give you a present. I'm sure I have something in my cave you'd like."

Anatole was so thankful not to be eaten up that he did not run. The Blimlim flashed away into the darkness, and soon there came the clatter of somebody opening and shutting many doors.

"Are you still there?" called the Blimlim.

"Yes," Anatole called back.

Instantly the Blimlim reappeared, carrying a cup and saucer on its head.

"Perhaps you'd like some tea," it suggested. It lifted one wing, and out dropped a canister of Earl Grey tea. "Or don't you like tea? What do you like?"

"Ginger ale," said Anatole.

"To tell you the truth, I don't like tea, either. Wait. Don't go away."

It flickered out of sight and returned bearing a pair of sneakers in one claw and a dump truck in the other.

"These look about your size," it said cheerfully.

"Why, there's my truck," exclaimed Anatole, "and those are my sneakers! Where on earth did you find them?"

"The tide washed them in," answered the Blimlim. "Every morning I comb the beach for treasures. Sometimes I throw things back." The Blimlim flung the tea canister high into the sky. "When I throw them with all my might, they don't return."

They both watched the canister disappear over the horizon.

"A penny for your thoughts," hissed the Blimlim.

"I was thinking that the emperor has offered half his kingdom for your skin," said Anatole.

The Blimlim snorted.

"My skin won't fit him," it said scornfully. And then its green skin turned pale as water.

"Did you come here to capture me?"

"HE SCRAMBLED TO HIS FEET AND THERE, WAITING TO BE NOTICED, CROUCHED THE BLIMLIM."

"No," said Anatole. "I came to see the garden and the golden bough."

"Oh, it's a lovely garden," exclaimed the Blimlim, much relieved. "Let me take you there. Climb on my head."

Clutching his sneakers and his dump truck, Anatole climbed into the space between its ears, where he could not help noticing how much its gold filigree crown resembled his grandmother's lost candy dish. The Blimlim glided into a hedge that clicked shut behind them, like teeth locking together.

"Now," whispered the Blimlim proudly as he lowered his head for Anatole to dismount, "look!"

Above the water, which gushed from a crystal grotto, the golden bough rose straight up like a tree of heaven. It gave off a light so brilliant that Anatole had to shade his eyes. The leaves did not shake and sigh in the wind, for there was no wind. All around the tree glowed beds of daffodils and roses, lilies and marigolds, and fruit trees of every kind.

"The golden bough grows only in this garden," said the Blimlim. "If you moved it, the bough would die. Tell me, have you ever seen marigolds to equal these? Each flower is a perfect topaz."

Anatole touched one, then drew his hand away, for the flowers felt cold and hard.

"They're all right, but you should smell the marigolds in my grandmother's garden."

"And these apples," continued the Blimlim. "Giant

rubies. They never lose their beauty. Do you like rubies?"

"Rubies are O.K.," agreed Anatole, "but you should taste the apples in my grandmother's garden. So juicy and sweet, I wish I had one right now. But your garden is very nice, too," he added hastily, for he was afraid of hurting the Blimlim's feelings.

"Yes, indeed, it's a lovely garden," said the Blimlim.

"But lonely, maybe," said Anatole.

The Blimlim sighed. "Very lonely. I'd move to the mainland at once if I could find a nice dark space where nobody would disturb me."

"I know of a nice dark space," said Anatole.

"Where?"

"Under my bed."

"Does anyone live there?" asked the Blimlim.

"I don't know. I'm afraid to look."

"You needn't be afraid if I'm there. Is it quiet?"

Anatole thought about this.

"I guess so. Grandma never cleans under the bed since she lost the mop."

"Did you say a mop?" exclaimed the Blimlim. "I found a mop not long ago."

"You did?"

"But I don't seem to remember where I put it," murmured the Blimlim nervously.

Silence fell, the silence of two friends who enjoy each other's company even when they are not conversing.

"When shall we leave?" asked Anatole at last.

"When your friends leave, we'll leave, too. Climb on my head."

The Blimlim streaked through the forest, its scales throwing sparks, and stopped behind the fountain of Venus, where the party of merrymakers thought they had just seen a rush of fireflies. In the twilight Anatole could make out the shadows of his friends: Thérèse's quick shadow, Gilles' drooping silhouette, and Madame d'Aulnoy's majestic shape, as large and elegant as a tree. They huddled around the ship as the Emperor of the Moon led the way on board, and their voices carried clearly.

"A pity about Frère Jacques," said Gilles. "He was a good-hearted fellow. I liked him."

"Perhaps the Blimlim has not eaten him," said Madame d'Aulnoy. "Perhaps he's found the golden bough."

And then Thérèse's voice: "How dark it is! Isn't it time to light the lamps?"

Lanterns twinkled at stem and stern. Even after the ship sailed out of sight, Anatole, left behind on the dark shore, could hear the frail music of their laughter.

"They're gone," said the Blimlim with a sigh. "Do you know the way back to your country?"

"That way," said Anatole, and he pointed into the darkness.

"You are pointing to the end of the world," said the Blimlim. "If you're wrong, we will fall off the earth, and who knows what will become of us?"

"It may be the end of the world," said Anatole, "but that is where I live."

"Very well," said the Blimlim. "Hang on tight."

And it plunged into the black water and swam straight into the moonless night, with Anatole on its head. Its body cut the water like a skillfully guided blade, scarcely disturbing it, making no noise and no waves. Neither spoke for a long time.

Suddenly the Blimlim shuddered. "I say, look there. Do you see a tree?"

"Where?" cried Anatole.

"Just in front of us."

Anatole clapped his hands.

"That's our hatrack! That's Grandpa's cap and that's Jon's umbrella and there's Grandpa's old sweater hanging on it. We're nearly home. We're headed for the front hall."

To avoid a collision, the Blimlim passed behind the mirror and the telephone stand and sailed upstairs. Suddenly all its scales stood on end.

"Hark! I hear the clash of weapons. Are we in enemy waters?"

"The clash of weapons? Oh, that's our radiators turning on. Nothing to worry about. This is Grandma's dressing table."

They brushed his grandmother's perfume bottles and slipped behind the headboard of her bed, gliding behind Grandpa's bed and round the other side. The Blimlim sniffed his hand as it lay on the covers. Grandpa opened his eyes and waved as Anatole and the Blimlim blew across the hall.

Through the open door he saw his mother's dolls smiling at him from their high shelf and Jon asleep in the rocker beside the bed.

"Do you see that dark space there?" asked Anatole, pointing. "That's your house."

Swish! The Blimlim darted out of the wallpaper and disappeared under the bed, dropping Anatole head first into the blankets. His sneakers and his dump truck clattered to the floor.

"Aggggg," yawned Jon.

Anatole hung his head over the side of the bedclothes and whispered, "Blimlim! How do you like it?"

"Comfy," answered a voice thick with dust. "You're not scared anymore, are you?"

"No," said Anatole.

"What a relief not to be guarding treasure! Wake me up if you need my help."

"Do you want anything to eat?"

"Eat!" exclaimed the Blimlim. "I'm much too old for such dependencies."

Jon stirred again. Anatole scooted under the covers and pretended to be asleep as Jon rubbed his eyes, scratched his back, gazed around him in bewilderment, and tiptoed out of the room.

Thump! Grandma's feet struck the floor. Anatole

"GRANDPA OPENED HIS EYES AND WAVED AS ANATOLE AND THE BLIMLIM
BLEW ACROSS THE HALL."

jumped out of bed. He could hear water running in the bathroom. Grandpa was sitting on the edge of the bathtub. Bzzzz! whined the electric razor as Grandma ran it over his cheek.

"Good morning," said Grandma. "Try to be quiet, will you? Jon fell asleep in his chair, and he's stiff as starch. He's gone back to bed."

Bzzz! sang the razor over Grandpa's chin.

"I saw Anatole this morning in the wallpaper," said Grandpa.

Grandma snapped off the razor and kissed his ear.

"Of all the nonsense I ever heard, that takes the cake. But, Anatole, guess what I found under the bathroom sink? My tea canister."

"Did you, Grandma?"

"And guess what else I found? Kneel down here and look."

Together they crouched under the sink. Grandma pointed to the place where the pipe joined the wall.

"A garden in the wallpaper," she exclaimed. "I never saw it before. Look, here's an apple tree and some yellow violets—"

"Those are marigolds, Grandma," said Anatole, "not violets."

His grandmother studied them.

"So they are," she agreed. "I wish I could pick some. I bet they'd smell nice."

"They don't smell at all," said Anatole. "They're made of topaz."

"Topaz, indeed," snorted Grandma. "How do you know they're made of topaz?"

"I touched them," said Anatole.

The Island of the Grass King

"ON THE BACK OF THE GREAT DANE RODE AN OLD WOMAN
IN A GREEN CLOAK..."

I.

Fennel," said Grandmother, "if I only had my fennel back! It used to grow right here. I believe the winter killed it."

And breathing heavily, she sat down on the stone bench hidden among the larkspurs at the back of the garden. Anatole sat down beside her. It always alarmed him when she wheezed for breath, but he tried not to show his concern.

"Did you take your medicine, Grandma?"

Grandmother drew from her pocket a little bottle with a spout at one end and a bulb at the other. She held the spout to her mouth, pressed the bulb, and inhaled deeply. Then she held up the bottle to see how much was left.

"Nearly gone," she observed. "The doctor said I could only take it twice a day. It helps my breathing, but it can't be good for me. Now if he'd prescribed fennel tea, I could drink as much as I wanted. Fennel's an old cure for asthma."

"Can't you buy more fennel?" asked Anatole.

Grandmother brushed some dead leaves off the face of the sundial.

"No. Not like what I lost. Your grandpa got the seeds from his high school botany teacher, who got it from an island he once visited where fennel grew wild. Wild plants are best for healing. Well, nothing lasts forever, does it? How hot the sun is! I'm going indoors."

Anatole followed her to the back porch, and together they cleared the old magazines off the swing, leaving only Plumpet, Anatole's orange cat, snoozing at the foot. Grandma never allowed anyone to interrupt Plumpet's naps, and if the cat chose to curl up on Grandma's paper while she was writing a letter, she simply wrote around her, though it left a great hole in the middle of her letter, like this:

Dear Anna and Theo,

I hope you are en-joying your stay in London. Anatole and I are getting along famously. Today he vacuumed the downstairs while I made a lemon pie. Then in the afternoon we went to a garage sale, and he bought a shoe box full of baseball cards for 25¢. And guess who he got? Babe Ruth!

Love,
mother

Grandma sat down on the swing and closed her eyes. Anatole sat down beside her and did not close his, for over the back of the swing hung a map of the world, and he enjoyed finding all the places he would visit someday. First he found England, because his parents were there right now, and just yesterday he had gotten a postcard from his papa with a picture of the Queen on it.

Then he found Florida, where Grandma spoke of going for the winter, but never did. The brown-winged splotch that lay just north of Florida and south of Bermuda puzzled him, for it did not seem to be one of the real places that had names. And there were odd streaks to the west of Puerto Rico, where the rain had leaked in through the roof once and left its footprints on everything.

Far away the sky rumbled. Anatole sat up and peered through the screens to see if a storm was gathering, but the evergreens and wisteria grew so thickly around the porch that he could see nothing but leaves and the leaves' shadows, which brushed like lace over the floor.

Grandmother opened her eyes.

"Listen."

"Thunder," said Anatole.

"Mother Weather-sky is moving her furniture," said Grandmother. "She's never satisfied with the present arrangements."

Suddenly a great crack of thunder shook everything, and the rain seemed to burst from the clouds. It roared like a drumroll on the eaves-trough overhead, yet the lacy shadows on the floor did not fade.

"Rain and sun together," said Grandmother. "That means a rainbow. I haven't seen one for ages."

"I've never seen a rainbow," said Anatole. "I mean, not in the sky," he added, for his mother had shown him the earth rainbows that lazed in puddles on the road after a storm, and his father had shown him the small rainbows stirred up by the lawn sprinkler and had told him they didn't come from the hose.

"Perhaps big rainbows are extinct," said Grandmother. "I used to wish on the big rainbows. Or perhaps there's one just behind those trees."

"Can we wish on it even if we can't see it?" asked Anatole.

"Of course we can. I wish that my housework would do itself tonight."

Anatole did not tell his wish, for fear it would not come true.

"And can Plumpet make a wish too?" he asked. "Only I'll have to make it for her. I suppose she would like to talk our language, so she could tell you when she's hungry."

"She does quite well already," said Grandmother. "In the meantime, while we are waiting for miracles, we have the Sears Roebuck catalogue to wish on."

Grandma kept the catalogue by the swing so that she and Anatole could consult it when they wanted to make wishes. Now they leafed through the toy section, page by page, deciding what they would like to have most. Grandma chose for herself a lovely bride doll, which she said she had always dreamed of as a child but never owned. Anatole chose the disguise kit. Then, as a favor to Grandmother, he turned to the section on kitchenwares, but he was so long in finding the page on dishwashers that when he was ready to make his wish, he found Grandmother had fallen asleep.

He laid the catalogue on the floor and tiptoed indoors. From the dining room table rose the dark shapes of teapots, urns, and pitchers. He and Grandma had found them all this very morning after his ball rolled under the guest-room bathtub, and they'd both scrambled down on their hands and knees to fetch it. First he found a harmonica with dust in its teeth.

"That belonged to your mother," said Grandmother. "She used to play 'Yankee Doodle' on it while she stirred the cheese sauce on the days I made broccoli for supper. I didn't know it was still in the house."

"Can I have it?" asked Anatole.

Grandma nodded and put it in his pocket. Then suddenly they both spied something round and flat under the tub, and Grandma gave a shout of joy.

"So that's where I hid the silver! It's been missing for two years."

And she pulled out a platter and half a dozen forks and a short squat coffeepot. The coffeepot had feet, three of them, which ended rather ominously in claws. Anatole did not believe these things could be real silver—they looked so dark—but he carried them downstairs anyway. And when Grandma brought out the tin of polish and two polishing cloths, he set to work and soon saw how much lay hidden under the heavy tarnish.

But they hadn't finished, and the coffeepot had one bright side and one dark side. Anatole took up the cloth and, feeling very helpful, began to rub away at a spot on the dark side of the coffeepot. And now a curious thing happened. The more he rubbed, the more he saw. Leaves appeared here, flowers there, and a dozen animal faces behind them, till he believed he was looking into a forest in which the sun was just rising.

He was so busy that he did not hear Grandmother come up behind him.

"...WHEN HE WAS READY TO MAKE HIS WISH, HE FOUND
GRANDMOTHER HAD FALLEN ASLEEP."

"What a wonderful discovery! I never knew there were so many creatures on that old coffeepot."

"Can we eat off these dishes tonight?" asked Anatole.

"You can," said Grandmother. "They're too fancy for me."

"But you bought them!"

"No, I didn't. When your father's great-aunt died, all her things were sent to us. She bought those dishes. You can't imagine the number of curiosities we received when she died. The only one I like is the barometer. It really works."

And from the top of the china cabinet she lifted something that looked like a clock with only one hand. Its numbers were in all the wrong places, and it was set in the belly of a white pig.

"I wish I had a barometer," said Anatole, who was fond of pigs.

"When the needle moves to the left, it's a storm. To the right—"

Suddenly a clap of thunder shook everything. And Grandmother, as if it had been a bell, said, "Time for supper."

They ate peanut butter sandwiches in the kitchen on the dropleaf table that wiggled if you leaned on it too hard, and Grandmother tried in vain to pry open a jar of strawberry preserves, remarking all the while on the obstinacy of inanimate things. And then they listened to the rain turning itself on and off, till the windows grew quite dark. Anatole took out the harmonica and tried

"Yankee Doodle." Grandmother listened gravely. By the time he reached the last line he was winded.

"You play almost as well as your mother did," she observed. "I could always tell how she was feeling by the music she played. She used to play 'Ruby' when she was feeling low. Do you know 'Ruby'?"

"No," said Anatole. "Is it harder than 'Yankee Doodle'?"

"It's slower but longer," said Grandmother. "It was popular once, in certain circles."

When they had cleared the table and rinsed the dishes, Grandmother helped Anatole make up the sofa in the living room. Though there were plenty of beds in the house, he liked the sofa best of all. He did not ask her to tell him a story, though she told lovely stories. His mother had warned him not to give Grandma extra trouble in any way. So he said, "Do you have any nice picture books I can read tonight?"

"What kind do you want tonight?"

"I want another book about monsters."

"I think we have found all the monster pictures in the *National Geographic*, but I have another book you might like just as well," said Grandmother, and she disappeared into the sunroom.

When she came back, she was holding a fat book bound in brown leather and tooled with gold. "Did I ever tell you why we were so poor when I was little? My father was a doctor, and if people couldn't pay him in money, he'd let them pay him in whatever way they could. He once treated a man who lived in a castle. You'd think a man who lived in a castle could pay his bills. But no, he gave my father this book about a man who goes on a long journey. When I was a child, my sisters and I mapped out the whole journey in our backyard. And how the patients used to stare when we said, 'Look out! You're walking on the Enchanted Ground!' or 'Watch your footing, that's the Hill of Difficulty!' for there was nothing to be seen but the asparagus patch and the front steps."

And she opened the book to a picture of a dragon breathing fire and smoke on a very small man standing just at the edge of its enormous paws. Plumpet jumped on Anatole's lap, as if she wanted to look also.

"Have you any monsters in this house?" asked Anatole.

"We'll go exploring one of these days and find out," said Grandmother.

"Can I keep Plumpet with me tonight?" asked Anatole, hoping Grandmother wouldn't put her outside, for sometimes she roamed about the house at night, pouncing on moths. She never caught the moths but she always woke up Grandmother.

"Plumpet, you take care of Anatole," said Grandmother. "Make sure he brushes his teeth."

Anatole brushed his teeth, but he forgot to change from his shorts to his pajamas and to take his sneakers off, and by the time he remembered, he was too sleepy to care. He looked for a few minutes at the pictures in the book; then he stretched out his arm to the table behind him and turned out his light.

But the moon did not turn off hers. For a few minutes Anatole heard Grandma coughing upstairs. Then silence seemed to fill the house from top to bottom. Even Plumpet had stopped purring, but she warmed Anatole's feet with her stomach, and he was glad for her company. If he were home, his mother would come to him and sing his favorite song about the boy who played the harmonica so well that he was king of the world. *Every thing that heard him play* (here she would tuck him in), *even the billows of the sea* (here Plumpet would jump on the bed), *hung their heads and then lay by* (here she would turn off the hall light and he would begin to feel sleepy).

He did not feel sleepy now. He glanced into the round mirror over the fireplace and saw the dining room. The moon was shining through the French door at the far end.

Presently he heard voices. Glancing again at the mirror, he thought he saw lights moving across its pale surface. Very quietly he got up and crossed to the door that joined his room to the other and peered between the hinges. What he saw astonished him.

A teapot was rolling in the silver polish like a pig in a puddle, and the forks were scrubbing each other with their prongs, and the platter was shouting angrily to the dishes in the kitchen. Anatole crept around the door and edged out till he had a good view of the kitchen. The glasses from which he and Grandma had drunk lemonade only a few hours before were dancing in the sink, and the plates were all lined up on the drainboard singing:

"The kettles and the dishes,
they rule the happy home.
Of all the rooms in Grandma's house,
the kitchen wears the crown."

"So Grandma got her wish!" exclaimed Anatole to himself.

An old skillet caught sight of him and nudged him out of his hiding place.

"He shall settle it! He shall settle it!"

And hearing that someone of importance had arrived, the cups and glasses and plates marched from the kitchen and assembled themselves around Anatole. There was something especially touching about the cups, for every one had a chipped lip or a handle broken off, and they stood as proudly as soldiers who have come through a great battle.

"Well, which of us wears the crown?" asked the skillet. "The silver dishes, spoiled things, who never do a lick of work, or the good folk of the kitchen, who really earn their keep and are thrown into the garbage at the end of their lives?"

Anatole was about to say that the silver did very well for company dinners and the kitchen dishes were awfully noble to help out the rest of the time, but before he could find words, a great light flooded the room, and all the dishes turned around to see where it came from. Beyond the French door, the moon had gotten itself tangled in Grandma's clothesline.

"Look!" said Plumpet. "There in the yard!"

It was not the moon that sent such brightness everywhere, but something enormous that shook the light off its wings like drops of rain. Anatole pulled back the latch on the door and ran outside in time to see the wings rise and fall and disappear behind Grandma's broken-down garage.

2.

Even during the day, Anatole stayed clear of the dark passage behind Grandma's garage. The neighbors who lived in back of Grandma piled their old leaves and grass cuttings there. Nettles and Virginia creeper grew in all directions. An abandoned lilac bush had long ago shut out the sunlight, making the place a perfect garden of toadstools. The car in Grandma's garage had been driven by Grandpa before he died. Grandma did not like machines. She did not know how to drive, and she kept the car only for sentiment. Through the broken slats in the back wall, one could see old mowers, scythes, bottles. Mildew spotted everything.

At the edge of the dark yard, Anatole paused. He thought once more of the wings and the extraordinary brilliance they had shaken on the grass, the clothesline, the dining room floor. Then he crept around the corner of the garage and held his breath.

On the heap of dead leaves stood a giant horse. It was as high as the garage, and as gray as a stormy sky, and it was fanning its wings back and forth, stirring the leaves and brushing away the toadstools. With every pulse its wings scattered a burst of light, and the nettles shone— now red, now green, now blue, now silver.

"So you see," said the horse, as if resuming an old conversation, "rainbows are not extinct. My brothers and I often come here, but your grandma never prunes her shrubs, so she never sees the rainbow anymore."

"Are you the rainbow?" asked Anatole.

"No, indeed. There is only one rainbow in the sky, and the rain lets people see it in different places, at different times. I know this, for I live at the top of it when I am not visiting the earth. Nice garden, your grandmother's. I saw you sitting with her this afternoon."

"I didn't see you," said Anatole.

"No," said the horse. "My brothers and I, we keep to ourselves."

"Then why can I see you now?"

"ON THE HEAP OF DEAD LEAVES STOOD A GIANT HORSE."

"Because you wished that Grandma might get her fennel back, and I've come to take you to the place where it grows wild. Are you ready to leave?"

Anatole clapped his hands.

"Oh, yes! Is it far?"

"Very far," answered the horse.

He lowered his head and turned over a dead leaf with his hoof. "I don't suppose you've got a few oats in the house you could spare? It's no trouble to you, this journey. You have nothing to do but sit on my back. As for me—"

"Just a minute," said Anatole, and he ran across the wet grass into the house.

The pots and pans and plates, huddled at the French door with their spouts and handles pressed to the glass, crowded around him.

"What did you see? What did you see?"

"I found a horse," said Anatole, making a path through them. "A rainbow horse. And he's going to show me where Grandma's fennel went, and she'll be well again. Let me by."

They followed him into the kitchen, shouting and clamoring as he climbed up on a stool and searched the cupboard for the oatmeal. Then he remembered that Grandma had used it to make granola. So he took down the jar of granola, which smelled sweetly of almonds and honey, and he was about to carry it out to the horse when a voice said, "And what will Grandma eat for her breakfast?"

Glaring at him from the top of the breadbox was a crouched Plumpet. The silver coffeepot was knocking against Anatole's shins, demanding to be heard, and the boy seized it and shouted, "Now be still, you stupid thing!" and he poured it half full of granola. Then he pushed the jar back on the shelf and hurried outside with all the pots and dishes clattering at his heels, and he held up the silver coffeepot to the horse.

The horse dipped his nose into it, sighed with pleasure, and did not lift his head till he had eaten down to the very bottom.

"Fine oats," he murmured. "The earth always gives me such an appetite." And he bent one huge wing and swept Anatole onto his back.

"Are you ready?" asked the horse again.

"Yes," said Anatole. Something thumped down behind him.

"I'm coming to take care of you," purred Plumpet, settling herself at his back. "I promised your grandmother, you know."

With a rush of wind the horse rose straight into the air, and whether they passed through the leaves or around them, Anatole did not know. He only clung to the horse's mane and closed his eyes.

"Look down," said Plumpet. "What a fine sight."

Below them, Grandma's house and the road on which it stood were growing smaller and smaller. Now they were passing the dairy at the edge of town. The cows huddled in the yard, the milk trucks were just setting out into the dark, but from where he sat Anatole could see the sun pushing its shafts of light across the earth as if it were raking the houses and fields together.

"Why, you've brought the coffeepot!" exclaimed Plumpet.

Anatole looked down and, sure enough, nestled under his arm was the silver coffeepot, one side shiny, one side still dark, for he had never finished polishing it. He held it up to his ear, but to Anatole's relief it behaved like an ordinary pot, neither speaking nor moving. For the first time he wondered where he was going.

Leaning forward, he put his mouth to the horse's ear, which was as soft as violets, and he called, "Where will I find the fennel?"

"You will find it in Mother Weather-sky's garden," answered the horse.

"Are you taking me to her?"

The horse grew stubborn and would not answer. At last he said, "When the Roadkeeper asks you your destination, just tell him you are going to see Mother Weather-sky."

"And will Mother Weather-sky be glad to see me?" asked Anatole.

Again the horse fell silent, and when he finally spoke, his voice sounded sad and far away.

"Well, I'm bound to tell you, she doesn't like visitors."

Anatole started to ask why, but the cat interrupted him. "Look down, look down!"

Under the horse's hooves the clouds broke, and a

handful of islands floated like leaves on bright water. He recognized Florida and the thin curve of Cuba, Santo Domingo to the south and Puerto Rico farther south yet, and all by itself to the north a peppering of very tiny islands. Those were the Bermudas.

The horse dipped closer to the water below, and the boy watched the waves roll, gather themselves into hills of green glass, and break into pieces. In the rising of the waves he could see what each was carrying. One hauled a glittering load of compasses, another half a dozen chairs, a third the sails of a ship. The largest looked quite empty, yet when it broke, Anatole heard the cries of drowning men, and he turned quickly away, for fear that he would see their bones in the wave that followed.

All around them, clouds swelled into monstrous creatures, dragons with spiked tails and needle-sharp whiskers, ogres with huge mouths and a single eye or with eight eyes and a single foot. Though Anatole had often amused himself finding monsters in the clouds, he had never imagined them close up. They floated by him, still and blind as statues, terrible to look at but harmless.

"They are all asleep," said the horse, "but when they wake up, watch out!"

"Can they hurt us?" asked Anatole.

"They can't hurt me," said the horse. "If lightning hits me, I break apart and come together again."

Anatole thought uneasily of the voices in the wave.

"Are we close to the island?"

"Why, it's just below us!"

"I can't see anything but water below us," said Anatole.

"That's all you can see from the outside. But when I've put you on the island, I promise you'll see it plain enough. I can't talk any more now, for the clouds are stirring themselves."

The horse moved very slowly between the monsters, as if the air itself weighed him down. When Anatole bumped his elbow against a two-headed elephant, he found to his surprise that it was soft and boneless, like smoke. The beast opened its eyes, stared at Anatole, lifted its trunks, and trumpeted.

At once the other beasts opened their eyes and, catching sight of the boy and the horse, rolled toward them, raising a cold wind that blew the travelers helplessly this way and that.

"The storm has caught us," called the horse over his shoulder. "Jump off!"

"No!" shouted the cat and the child together.

"Jump off, I say! Quickly!—"

Suddenly the dragon opened its mouth and shot out a long tongue of fire, and Anatole felt the horse shatter like crockery under him, and he saw the shimmering wings sail away by themselves into the sky. The next minute he landed not on the waves but on the island, just as the horse had promised.

3.

he storm was gone. The sky, washed clean, shone blue as a bunting's wings. Waves lapped at Anatole's feet and terns skittered along the bright lip of the water.

Plumpet was washing vigorously behind her ears.

"Salt," she said. "I am sure it was the salt in the sea that saved us. I've seen your mother toss a pinch of salt over her left shoulder when she spills it, and she won't do as much for pepper or cinnamon." Stretching herself lazily, she added, "Did you bring the map? I would like to know where we are."

"So would I," said Anatole.

Before them glittered the sand. Behind them rose a thicket of wild sea grapes, and beyond the thicket were the dark crowns of pines, as tall as steeples. Anatole shaded his eyes and looked up and down the beach. Nobody was coming or going in either direction, but off to the left, where the water met the land, stood a little telescope on a tripod that might have been gold once but now wore a heavy coat of barnacles. Kicking off his sneakers, Anatole ran down the beach and put his eye to the lens. Though he turned it this way and that, he saw nothing but darkness. When he tried to pull it up, the tripod seemed to take root in the sand. Disappointed, he walked back to Plumpet. Over his shoulder he saw the waves licking up his footprints as the telescope sank slowly into the sea.

"The tide is coming in," observed Plumpet. "Listen."

A bell sounded, so far off and mournful that Anatole shivered. It might have been a buoy or a lighthouse warning some passing ship of danger. It rang once more, this time in a high sweet voice like a chime, and as if answering a summons, a small shiny creature scuttled out of the thicket and rubbed itself joyfully against the boy's legs.

"Oh, it's Grandmother's coffeepot!" he cried. "How glad I am that I didn't lose it!"

And the coffeepot shook itself like a dog and trotted round and round on little silver paws, opening and shutting its lid for joy.

The bell sounded a third time. Grabbing his shoes, Anatole climbed the sloping beach to the thicket, for now he was sure the bell had rung from that direction. The branches parted themselves and showed him a tunnel that led straight into the thicket. The sun slipping in and out of the leaves threw emerald lights along the path, and the air was the color of Plumpet's eyes.

"It's almost as if someone were expecting us," said Anatole.

Plumpet put her nose in the tunnel and caught the scent of freshly buttered toast.

"Then we'd better not keep them waiting," she purred and darted down the green path ahead of him.

The leaves gave off a delicious fragrance, rather like cloves, and Anatole was not surprised to hear the steady hum of bees all around him. The coffeepot, stumbling along on its short legs, could not keep up. Anatole tucked it under his arm and hurried after Plumpet. Ahead of them, at the far end of the tunnel, they saw a cave. A ring of candles hung from the ceiling and spread its warm light over a round table, covered with a blue-checkered tablecloth. On the table, someone had carefully arranged four white napkins rolled into gold napkin rings, four teacups, four gold spoons, four gold knives, and a porcelain teapot, white as a new tooth, from which steam rose. And in the middle of it all was a plate of freshly buttered toast.

"Why, we're in somebody's dining room!" exclaimed Anatole.

Around the table stood three stools and a baby's high chair with MIRANDA lettered in gold on the back. But the walls of the cave were all given over to cupboards and drawers. A low door at the back led off into darkness.

"Perhaps a monster lives here," said Anatole.

"Perhaps it doesn't," said Plumpet. "I'm famished."

"I suppose we shouldn't sit down till we're asked," said Anatole, hoping Plumpet would tell him it was all right, when you were very hungry, to eat first and be asked later. She always did the correct thing.

Suddenly footsteps on dry twigs crackled from the back of the cave. Plumpet sprang to Anatole's shoulder in alarm.

Out of the darkness stumbled a little man. He was not much taller than Anatole, yet he looked old enough to be his great-grandfather, and he was pulling his beard out of his suspenders, which shone like a pair of matched rainbows on his leather shirt, the color of dead leaves. Anatole shrank back, but the old man did not notice.

"Wonderful to see you," he greeted them, "simply wonderful. It's been ages since I've had a visitor. Usually *she* gets them before I do. I've had the table set for centuries. I *hope* the tea is still hot." He clasped the teapot in both hands. "Names! Names!" Turning to the coffeepot nestled in Anatole's arms, he shook his finger at it. "You! Potiphar!"

The pot did not budge.

"Not Potiphar? The Lord of Sheffield!"

Still the pot did not move.

"Not Sheffield, either? Quicksilver, then. Is your name Quicksilver?"

At that the coffeepot leaped into the highchair and drummed its spout on the tray.

"And you?" said the old man, in a softer voice, looking from the cat to the boy and back again.

"My name is Anatole."

"Plumpet here," said the cat. She thought the old man very clever for having guessed the name of the coffeepot, when she hadn't known it had one all the years it lived in Grandmother's house.

"We're delighted to meet you, Mr.—" She glanced at the name on the high chair—"Mr. Miranda."

The old man laughed.

"I'm not Mr. Miranda. I don't even know Miranda. Was she a puppy? A lizard? A bird? I found all the furniture in the cave when I moved in. The tide rushed into my old cave and carried everything away. Here now, we'll have a party in honor of your arrival."

By the light of the candle, Anatole caught a glimpse of animals painted on the ceiling, mostly reindeer and buffalo. The light gliding across them made them appear to be running away.

"Where are we?" asked Plumpet. Her voice trembled a little.

"You are on the island of Sycorax," replied the old man. "Do sit down."

When they were seated at the table, he helped them all

to tea and toast—even the coffeepot, who sucked the tea into its spout like an anteater and shot it high into the air like a whale. And how skillfully it opened its lid and caught every drop!

"What a pity the tea doesn't come in bags with fortunes on the tags," Anatole whispered to Plumpet. "In a place like this, I am sure all the fortunes would come true."

"It is a pity," said the old man, "and we have no music. Can you sing, boy?"

"No, but I can play the harmonica," said Anatole, and he took it out of his pocket and played "Yankee Doodle." The old man listened, cocking his head to one side like a bird.

"Did you get it from the sea?" he asked.

"No, from my grandmother."

"I hope everything is satisfactory?" he continued.

Anatole helped himself to a second piece of toast.

"It's very good, thank you," he said. "Do you often have visitors here?"

The old man shook his head.

"Mostly I sleep. I might sleep a hundred years, I might sleep an hour. I sleep till I'm wanted. My telescope watches for visitors, and when I'm wanted, it rings me awake. People come, they eat my bread and drink my tea, and they go on their way."

"Doesn't anybody ever stay?" asked Anatole.

"Nobody," answered the old man. "All the folks that come to me are looking for something. So are you. And

"'NO, BUT I CAN PLAY THE HARMONICA,' SAID ANATOLE, AND HE TOOK IT
OUT OF HIS POCKET AND PLAYED 'YANKEE DOODLE.'"

wherever you're going you'll need a road to take you there. That's my business. Roads."

"Do you sell maps?" inquired Plumpet.

"I sell roads," said the old man. "When this island was young and nameless, you could find roads everywhere. They'd be floating on every stream and hiding under every stone. Mother Weather-sky and her sisters collected them all and made me Keeper of the Roads. I don't keep them, though. I sell them."

"Won't you run out of roads someday?" asked Anatole.

"No, for they always come back to me when travelers are done with them."

"In my country," said Anatole, "the roads stay where they're put."

"A poor sort of arrangement," said the old man. "Look here."

He gestured toward the hundreds of drawers niched in the wall around them.

"Do you know what I keep in these?" he demanded.

"Buttons?" suggested Anatole. They reminded him of the drawers in the sewing store where his mother bought buttons and embroidery thread.

"Buttons, indeed! This drawer is cut from a single ruby. And the one beside it, from a single emerald." And while the Keeper of the Roads praised them, they shone so brightly that you could have read a book by their light. "They hold roads. No two drawers are alike, and no two roads lead to the same place."

"What kind of road do you keep in here?" asked

Anatole, pointing to a drawer studded with opals. The fire in the stones shivered like lightning, as if the road inside were losing its temper. The Keeper of the Roads opened it and lifted out a golden chain, long and heavy and restless as a snake. It undulated nervously around his fingers, winding and unwinding.

"Nice to look at but cold to travel," he remarked. "Unfortunately it takes you to the most dangerous part of the island. Once it took travelers to and from a city of gold. Now the city is gone, but the road doesn't know that. Roads keep their old habits, you know."

And he coiled it up like a spring and popped it back into the drawer.

"What's in that diamond drawer?" asked Plumpet.

The Keeper of the Roads opened a crystal drawer and picked up a road that shone softly, like one long tear. Plumpet gave an involuntary purr.

"It's very attractive, isn't it?" agreed the Keeper of the Roads. "Oh, it takes you through some lovely places, but it ends badly. Where did you say you wanted to go?"

"We want to find Mother Weather-sky," said Anatole. "Have you a road that will take us to her?"

The Keeper of the Roads stopped smiling.

"I was afraid you would ask for that one. You don't look like the sort that travels the diamond way."

"Then you've got that road?" asked Anatole eagerly. When the old man hesitated, he added, "I don't have any money to buy it, but maybe I could earn the road? I'm a good weeder and raker—"

"No, no, my dear, I can't take anything for this road. It's so full of dangers I can't possibly give it to a child. To a soldier with a sharp sword, yes. To a strong man with a pride of lions to defend him, yes. To a wise man with a headful of lore and a handful of spells, yes. But to a child, no. Why do you want to find Mother Weather-sky?"

"I want her to give me some of her fennel. It's supposed to cure asthma."

"You don't look sick," observed the Keeper of the Roads. "You look in the very pink of health."

"Oh, I don't want it for myself," explained Anatole. "I want it for my grandmother."

The Keeper of the Roads sighed so heavily that the candles flickered.

"If you were traveling for yourself, I might turn your mind another way. But when people want a thing for somebody else, they'll never give up till they've found it. The road you need is in this drawer. No, not that amethyst one, this plain wooden drawer. Be patient, please, it always sticks."

The road to the garden was dull as dust and thin as snakeskin and so snarled you couldn't tell the end from the beginning. The Keeper of the Roads laid it on his open palm and blew on it. It didn't move.

"Let me warn you about this island," he said. "It's a shifty sort of place, full of fogs and storms, but when the fogs lift and the storms pass, how beautiful it is! That's Mother Weather-sky's work, of course. Everything that comes loose in her storms she keeps in her garden—

figureheads, fountains, flags—and her garden is vast. It's not a garden really—it's a grave. You won't find a single green thing growing in it."

"Then where *is* the garden?" cried Anatole.

"This whole garden was an island once," answered the old man. Once more he blew on the road, as if he were sighing over it. "Such a garden! It had the usual things, of course, garlic and roses and marigolds, but herbs that could work great magic grew here as well. The island attracted magicians the way a magnet attracts pins. Most of them came and went, and the sea washed away their runes and residences, for the sea is clean as your cat here, always licking and polishing. But long ago a magician more powerful than the rest was tossed ashore in a storm."

"Is he still here?" asked Plumpet, glancing around uneasily.

"No, that was a long time ago. He scrambled out with his black velvet suit on his back and the *Red Calfskin Book of Magic* under his arm. You've heard of that book, no doubt."

"No, I haven't," said Anatole.

"Indeed! The *Red Calfskin Book* is the most powerful book of spells ever made. The Magician—he never had another name that I know of—wrestled it at midnight from the ghost of a famous wizard, and the ghost tore away the cover and the first five pages and carried them away. In those days the island was ruled by the King of the Grass."

"Oh, I've heard of him," exclaimed Anatole. "The

King of the Grass—he's the grasshopper, isn't he? My grandmother is very fond of watching grasshoppers."

"I do not think the island of Sycorax was ever ruled by a grasshopper," said the old man. "I have often been told the King wore a crown of fennel. That would be difficult for a grasshopper."

"So that's where I must look for my fennel," said Anatole in a discouraged voice. But the old man took no notice.

"The Magician didn't like regular gardens. He liked things that lasted. He wanted a garden of gold. He wanted to be king so he could order his people to make him one, but they wouldn't have him. So he turned the houses into trees and the people into stones."

"And the King too?" whispered Plumpet, appalled.

"The King and his Queen he locked up in a golden tree in Mother Weather-sky's garden. I believe he gave the key to Mother Weather-sky; I have heard she wears it at her waist, night and day. He couldn't change the King and Queen into stones, because the spell he needed for that was on the first page of the magic book. Their child escaped, but nobody knows where."

"What happened to the Magician?" asked Anatole.

"Drowned," answered the Keeper of the Roads. "Mother Weather-sky whispered a tale of sunken treasure in his ear and blew him a broken ship. He'd scarcely mended it and hoisted sail when she raised a storm that sent ship, Magician, and book to the bottom of the sea. She likes to run things herself, you know."

"So to find the fennel, I have to free the King. And to free the King, I have to get the key from Mother Weather-sky."

"Exactly. And she'll do her best to destroy you."

A low rumbling, deep under the rocks, startled them. Quicksilver jumped out of the high chair and rubbed against Anatole's ankles.

"I think I should like to go home," said Plumpet.

The Keeper of the Roads reached over and scratched her between the ears.

"Don't be afraid. The island is full of noises. Sometimes a thousand twangling instruments will hum about your ears, and sometimes voices. And if you've waked after a long sleep, they'll make you sleep again. Anatole, take off your left shoe."

Anatole kicked off one sneaker and stood on his right foot like a water bird before the old man. The Keeper of the Roads knelt down, spat on the road, and stuck it to Anatole's bare heel. At once the road faded, growing paler and paler until it disappeared entirely.

"What happened to the road?" asked Anatole.

"It's invisible," replied the Keeper of the Roads. "That's the only kind of road I keep. Whoever carries an invisible road always gets to the end of it. The only danger is losing yourself."

"How can we lose ourselves if we keep to the road?" asked Plumpet.

"Why, you might start out as a cat and end up a feather.

You might start out as a boy and end up a bracelet of bright hair about a bone."

"How ghastly," exclaimed Plumpet.

"Watch out for wizards," continued the Roadkeeper. "Don't drink from strange wells. And lie low during storms."

"Watch out for wizards," repeated Anatole, "don't drink from strange wells, and lie low during storms. Is that all?"

"That's enough," said the Roadkeeper pleasantly.

"Just a minute," said Anatole. "How can we follow the road if we can't see it?"

"Oh, the island has plenty of roads of the ordinary sort, and there are any number of footpaths that will take you, sooner or later, to Mother Weather-sky's garden. Remember to ask directions of everyone you meet. Come, I'll show you the footpath into the forest. It branches out of my dining room to the west."

4.

The footpath led straight into the forest and wound its way between pines and oaks so tall that the tops looked as if they were holding up the sky. Light breathed in and out of the canopy of branches, squirrels called to each other on their precarious journeys, birds flooded the woods with songs, blackberries gleamed in the hedges and thickets. Anatole improvised a suitable celebration on his harmonica. It was the sort of time and place that made you glad to be alive. Walking made Anatole hungry.

"Oh, Plumpet, let's pick blackberries and have a picnic!"

"Berries are not to my taste," answered the cat. "A little mole or slice of freshly killed mouse—"

The boy made a face.

"I can't eat with you if you're going to slice a mouse."

"Then I shall dine privately," said Plumpet. Like a gloved hand, she slipped into the berry thicket, and a wise choice it was, for if she had not left the path, she would never have discovered the stream, running clear and cold between banks of wild thyme and spearmint. Crouching on the mint, she discovered russet-backed crayfish swaying in the water weeds and speckled trout keeping watch over their nests. All this she studied as a hungry customer studies a menu in a restaurant.

Anatole was so busy picking blackberries that he did not notice Plumpet when she returned, picking her teeth with a claw not her own.

"Young crabs," she purred. "Haven't had 'em in years. If you want a cool drink, follow me."

Pushing through the thicket after her, Anatole gave a cry of delight. Honeysuckle filled the copse with a heavy sweetness, everything under his feet was in flower, everything in the stream glistened. The rocks made a path of stepping stones to the opposite bank. Anatole was about to jump on the first one when Plumpet leaped to his shoulder.

"Hush! Mind the adder!"

Across the water, a hedgehog scurried into the reeds.

The birds fell silent. Quicksilver lifted his spout and made small snuffling sounds. Not three feet away from them, a coil of spotted gold darted from under a leaf and glided into the stream. Anatole picked up an acorn and tossed it after the snake. It missed—he was glad of that— and struck the earth like a bell.

"Buried treasure!" exclaimed Plumpet. She sprang to the spot and applied her claws. Anatole knelt beside her and pushed aside handfuls of dirt, but it was hard work and he made so little progress that he soon sat back on his heels to rest.

"What I need is a shovel," he said.

"What you need are claws," said the cat. "You're not properly equipped for a long journey. Ah, what's this? A nose?"

They both leaned forward. Poking up through the dirt was a nose about the size of Anatole's, only smooth and transparent and hard as crystal.

"Why, it's made of glass," said Anatole, astonished.

"Fancy following an acorn and finding a glass nose," said Plumpet. "Where there's a nose, there's a face, at least in most cases."

They dug more eagerly now. Quicksilver carried the dirt away as fast as they scooped it out. Next a glass cheek came into view, then two glass eyes, glass lips slightly parted, a chin of dimpled glass, a glass forehead, and a glass neck. The face that shone up at them was young, pretty, and perfect in every detail.

Anatole took a stick and pried free two shoulders.

They were covered with glass hair, finely etched into straight strands that fell on both sides of the face. Plumpet uncovered two glass arms, a glass bodice and a full glass skirt, and two glass feet without shoes. The whole figure was dressed in a long-sleeved glass frock, pleated at the waist, but otherwise so plain that the dead leaves on which she lay could be clearly seen, as though through a magnifying glass. Together the boy and the cat lifted the girl out of the earth and stood her up in the sunlight.

She was not much taller than Anatole, and she was perfectly clear, like a window, except for a little gold whistle embedded on the left side of her chest, where live children have hearts. Anatole couldn't help admiring the whistle. It was shaped like a blade of snake grass, the kind that makes a rude noise if you hold it tight across your mouth and blow, and it seemed to draw light to itself so that it glittered like a tiny sun. But to get the whistle, he would have to smash the girl, a thought he put out of his head at once.

"What shall we do with her?" asked Anatole.

"Wash her," answered the cat.

Together they lifted her very carefully and laid her in the water.

"Fetch leaves and we'll scrub her," said Plumpet, for whom cleanliness was next to godliness. Every morning she scrubbed behind her ears, even outside in the coldest weather. As Anatole stooped to gather leaves, a cry went up from the stream.

"Help me!"

Spinning around, he saw the girl staggering to her feet, pulling at bunches of reeds to raise herself from the water. He ran to her and stretched out his hand, and she grasped it in her own. Her touch sent chills through him, it was so hard and cold.

"You're alive!" cried Anatole.

The girl waded ashore and glanced from the boy to the trees to the water to the cat, up to the sky and down to the wet roots shining in the mud.

"What does that mean, 'alive'?" she asked.

"Why, it means to walk and talk and eat and breathe," said Anatole. He paused. He felt he was explaining it badly.

"And where did I come from?" she continued.

"We found you in the earth," said Plumpet.

"Where I came from didn't look a bit like where I am now. Was I alive in the earth?"

"You didn't look alive," said Anatole.

"You looked dead as a caught mouse," added Plumpet.

"Was I dead?" asked the girl.

"The question is, Were you ever alive?" said Plumpet. "You have to be alive before you can be dead."

"I think you were asleep," said Anatole.

This answer evidently pleased her, for the whistle at her heart glowed like the cold fire in Grandmother's opal ring. The girl walked up and down the banks of the stream, swinging her arms and admiring the way they caught the sunlight.

"Alive. I'm alive. So that's who I am."

"HE RAN TO HER AND STRETCHED OUT HIS HAND,
AND SHE GRASPED IT IN HER OWN."

"Oh, that isn't *who* you are," said Plumpet. "That's *what* you are. What we all are. You have your own name. I am Plumpet. This is Anatole."

"And that little shining one?"

"He's my coffeepot, Quicksilver."

"Such lovely names," said the girl with a sigh. "Where did you get them?"

"From Anatole," said Plumpet.

"From Mama and Papa," said Anatole.

"And Quicksilver?"

"From the Keeper of the Roads," said Anatole.

The girl looked thoughtful.

"*Anatole*," she said softly. "*Anatole*. I like your name best. Can I borrow it?"

"I don't think so," he answered, feeling perplexed. "Didn't your parents give you a name?"

Immediately he wished he had not asked. He was sure she had no parents, and now she would want to know what parents were, and even the simplest questions sounded hard when she asked them.

"Perhaps you could find your own true name, as cats do," said Plumpet. "When a kitten is given its true name, it is read to from the *Book of Names* that have done good service in the past. When the kitten sneezes, the name being read is its real name, known only among cats."

"But you don't have the *Book of Names* with you," said Anatole.

"My dear Anatole," said the cat, "I have stood godmother to many a kitten, and I know the book by heart. Let us all sit down, and I'll begin the list."

They seated themselves on the mossy upholstery of the roots.

"Tybalt, Tomasina, Tabitha."

Plumpet paused.

"She doesn't look like a Tabitha," said Anatole. "She looks like a Susannah."

He meant to say that she looked like a photograph of his great-aunt Susannah as a young girl, which he had often admired in his mother's album.

"Minette, Minousse, Mimi."

"How long does the list go on?" asked the girl.

"Till you sneeze," answered the cat.

"Sneeze soon, won't you?" said Anatole. "We've got a long journey ahead of us."

"What is a sneeze?" asked the girl.

"Your nose tickles, you open your mouth, you close your eyes, and your breath just explodes. You can't do it on purpose, so it's no use trying," he added, for the girl was wrinkling her nose and opening her mouth and making the most hideous faces.

"Do the dead sneeze?" she asked.

"Only the living sneeze," said the cat.

"Then I shall manage it. Go on with the list."

"Miez, Gilbért, Tom—"

"Tom isn't right for a girl," said Anatole. "I think Susannah—"

Suddenly an acorn crashed through the trees and chimed off the girl's left shoulder.

"I sneezed!" she shouted.

"That's not a sneeze," said Plumpet.

"Why not?" demanded the girl. "Why should we all sneeze the same way?"

The cat could think of no reply.

"What name was I saying?"

"I was saying Susannah," said Anatole.

That settled it. Her name was Susannah. And now that she was somebody, she wanted to know what business they had in the woods. Then Anatole explained they were on their way to Mother Weather-sky's, to free the King of the Grass. And when he found the King of the Grass, he would ask for some of the fennel that grew in his crown, and he would take it to his grandmother, who had said nothing would heal her half so well as a cup of tea brewed from that herb.

Susannah turned to Plumpet.

"And why are you going? Do you have a grandmother, too?"

"I was sent to take care of Anatole," purred the cat. "Of course, I also wanted to come for the adventure of it all. I plan to write my memoirs some day, and I intend to fill them with the most fabulous adventures. It would be nice if a few of them were true."

"I would like to meet the King of the Grass," said Susannah.

"Then come with us," said Anatole.

Susannah gave him such a grateful smile that he decided she wouldn't mind if he asked, "Why is that whistle inside you?"

Susannah glanced down at it and shrugged. "Don't other people have whistles?"

"It's not common," said Plumpet. "Some children swallow pins or pennies, but I never knew anyone who had a whistle for a heart."

"Now you know one," said Susannah.

They returned to the footpath and set out. Anatole tried to play "Yankee Doodle" on his harmonica, but the farther they walked into the woods, the more the harmonica played its own tunes. Finally, it refused to play anything that Anatole recognized, though he blew the right notes for the tunes he knew. Very soon the woods grew so dark that they could not see the path before them. Quicksilver took fright and darted between their legs. They walked only with great difficulty, for fear of treading on him. At last Anatole picked him up and carried him.

"It would be a terrible thing if Susannah tripped and smashed herself to smithereens," said Plumpet. "I feel sure some magic is at work. It's much too early for nightfall. Let's stop here and rest till the darkness passes."

"What if it doesn't?" inquired Anatole.

"My dear Anatole, I have known the nine kinds of darkness: the darkness of night, the darkness of evil, the darkness of sorrow—"

Her voice trailed off. The present darkness was making

her sleepy. Anatole found himself yawning as well. The last words he heard before his eyes closed were Plumpet's:

"—so you see, my dear Anatole, there is no kind of darkness that sooner or later isn't followed by light."

5·

've found two more!" shouted a voice.

Anatole opened his eyes. In the pale light of early morning, a dozen golden retrievers peered down at him, as if he were a fox they had just flushed out of the underbrush. Anatole was not afraid of dogs; he had often been knocked down by the golden retriever who lived next door to him at home, but he had never been at the center of a pack of dogs, and he did not like the way they showed their teeth.

"If they weren't standing on their hind legs," he said to himself, "they wouldn't be any taller than I am. So perhaps they're not as fierce as they look."

A Great Dane pushed his way through the pack, stretched out one paw, snapped a collar around Anatole's neck, and yanked him rudely to his feet. With his other paw he was leading Susannah by a leash. Anatole was dismayed to see that she wore a brass-studded collar exactly like his own. He glanced around for Plumpet, but she had disappeared.

The Great Dane pointed to Quicksilver, crouched in Anatole's arms.

"What do you call that one?" he barked.

"A coffeepot," answered Anatole.

"Collar it!" howled the Great Dane.

And two retrievers stepped forward and slipped a collar around the neck of the coffeepot.

The first rays of morning broke over the trees. Susannah glittered and the whistle at her heart glowed, now a soft yellow, now deepening like an ember to bright orange. The dogs drew back in surprise.

"Are you under enchantment?" inquired the Great Dane.

"What does 'under enchantment' mean?" asked Susannah.

"It means you have lost the face you were born with. Were you born a dog?"

Susannah shook her head.

"Or a lizard?"

"Certainly not a lizard."

"Perhaps a hedgehog?"

"I have never been a hedgehog," said Susannah.

The Great Dane shook his head at her.

"That's too bad," he said. "There's special consideration for creatures under enchantment. The Governor doesn't want to arrest anybody on false charges. He doesn't want to condemn a rabbit to thirty days in the dungeon and have him turn into a horse. Prisoners, march!"

The Great Dane pulled their leashes so hard that they were obliged to follow him. The rest of the dogs ran behind, yapping among themselves.

"But why can't you put the horse in jail?" asked Susannah.

"You can't imprison a horse when you have condemned a rabbit. Every creature in this kingdom gets a fair trial. The fourth prisoner says he's under enchantment; but if you ask me, he's just trying to help his case."

"Where is the fourth prisoner?" asked Anatole, afraid that Plumpet had not escaped after all.

"He's there in the clearing," answered the Great Dane.

Ahead of them, surrounded by bloodhounds, stood a rabbit, seven feet tall, with emerald green fur and hoops of gold that gleamed in the tips of both his ears. He wore purple silk trousers cut off at the knee, and a leather vest several sizes too small for him. His right leg was sound,

but his left leg was wood, and when he spied the Great
Dane pulling his prisoners, he thumped his wooden leg
till the ground shook, and hazelnuts clattered down on
the dogs like hail. Not a single prisoner was hit.

"Hey, friends, what are they hauling you in for?"
roared the rabbit.

"I don't know," said Anatole.

The Great Dane tied the rabbit's leash to Anatole's collar, so that the new prisoner now led the rest.

"Prisoners, march!" bawled the Great Dane.

With a deep sigh, the rabbit heaved forward, pulling
the others after him. Very soon a stone lodged itself in
Anatole's sneaker. "How much better to be made of glass
like Susannah, or silver like the coffeepot, and feel nothing," he said to himself. Violets, pansies, and daisies covered the path. The trees smelled of cinnamon and cloves.
Each growing thing had reached its perfection; soon the
blossoms on the wild cherry trees would drop, but now
they hung like creamy clouds under the beeches and
oaks. It was spring, it was summer, it was no season, it
was the best season of all.

"A penny for your thoughts," said the rabbit, "though
of course I haven't got a penny."

Anatole considered his thoughts and decided that the
pain in his neck and the ache in his feet weren't worth
even the promise of a penny. So instead, he said that he
and his friends were going to Mother Weather-sky's garden, to rescue the King of the Grass. And he told him
about the fennel that grew in the King's crown, and how

"AHEAD OF THEM, SURROUNDED BY BLOODHOUNDS, STOOD A RABBIT,
SEVEN FEET TALL, WITH EMERALD GREEN FUR AND HOOPS OF GOLD…"

he wanted to bring some to his grandmother, so that she would be well again. The rabbit looked very surprised.

"I had no idea you were on such an important expedition," he said. "I assumed you were out for a walk." Then he added, "Good luck."

"Thank you," said Anatole.

"I'll bet you're wondering why I'm here," the rabbit went on. "Go ahead, ask me."

"Why are you here?" asked Anatole.

"I'm accused of stealing the lettuce from the Governor's royal gardens, which he grows to fatten rabbits for his table."

"And did you?" asked Anatole.

"I did. Oh, I'm guilty of that and a good deal more. But I'm sorry for you poor chaps. You're innocent."

"Then why did they capture us?" asked Susannah.

"Because you were sleeping next to me," said the rabbit.

"I didn't see you next to me," said Susannah, puzzled.

"Nor I you. But there we were, only a few feet apart, you on one side of the tree, I on the other. The dark spells that come over this forest have given me some strange bedfellows. I once spent the night not two feet away from an enormous dragon."

"And did you slay him?" asked Anatole, eager for a rousing story of conquest.

"No," answered the rabbit. "I ran. Lucky for me, I woke up first."

The memory of his escape pleased him so much that he began to sing, in a fine tenor voice that rang through the woods.

> "Shall Captain Lark the dragon slay?
> I came, I saw, I ran away."

"Is that your name? Captain Lark?" asked Susannah.

"At your service," said the rabbit. "Won't you give me yours?"

"I am Susannah. This is my friend Anatole. That's his coffeepot, Quicksilver."

"Susannah, Susannah," sang the rabbit softly. "You are the most beautiful lady in the woods. In fact, I think you're the only lady in the woods. Look sharp, friends. When we reach the rise, you'll see the Kingdom of the Dogs."

Over the top of the hill no trees grew, and the land dipped into a green valley, as round as a bowl. Anatole felt sure the grass had been mowed that morning, for he could smell wild onions and crushed clover, just as he smelled them at home after his papa had mowed the lawn. Around a cluster of low white houses ran a white picket fence, which did not look strong enough to keep anybody out. As the little party drew nearer, Anatole saw it was built of bones, polished white and studded with precious stones.

"How beautiful!" cried Susannah. "How the wall shines!"

"You would too," said Captain Lark, "if you wore all

that wealth. It's as stuffed with jewels as a plum cake with raisins. Pearls, sapphires, emeralds. They don't come out, though. I've tried to pry them loose. That ruby in the middle of the main gate would make your fortune."

The Great Dane ran forward and unlatched the gate.

"Where are we going?" asked Anatole.

"To the Governor's palace. Prisoners, march!"

"Just as if we could do anything else," whispered Susannah. "How he loves to order people about."

The Kingdom of the Dogs was not so tidy inside as it looked from a distance. The houses were shabby but well built, roofed with copper sheets that shone in the sun like a field of pennies. Some of the doorways were carved with fantastic beasts, and above the doors Anatole read the names of the families that lived behind them: *The Towsers, Old Tray, The Trot Family.* Between the houses, the grass lay trampled in curious swirls, as if some restless creature had turned itself round and round before falling asleep in it.

"Behold the garden of my undoing," said Captain Lark, pointing to a broad field of lettuce. "That's the Governor's royal garden."

"Where is everybody?" asked Susannah.

"Out of sight. It's considered bad luck to catch the eye of a prisoner, though if the Governor condemns us to death, you can be sure of a good crowd."

"He won't condemn us to death, I hope," said Anatole. Captain Lark shrugged.

"That depends on what kind of dog he is today."

"But isn't he always the same kind?" asked Anatole.

"He's never the same kind. He's the same dog, but never the same kind. Every morning he changes."

The Great Dane's ears twitched to show the prisoners he was listening to every word.

"But the punishment," said the Great Dane, "that doesn't change."

"What is the punishment?" asked Anatole.

"Death by the swing," said the Great Dane cheerfully. Seeing Anatole's bewildered expression, he added, "We have in our kingdom a swing that throws people into the sky. They never come down again."

Susannah turned to Captain Lark.

"Is this true?"

The rabbit nodded.

"I've heard of the swing, but I've never seen it. Only creatures condemned to death ever see the swing. The dogs who send them into the sky see it, of course. But they won't talk. Look sharp, children. Here's the Governor's palace."

It looked, thought Anatole, like his papa's toolshed, only much bigger. The front door was painted white and cut so exactly like a gravestone that he couldn't help looking for an inscription, and indeed he thought he saw a faint line of carved shapes that might have been letters when the door was new.

"I know it's a grand and fearful place," said the Great

Dane, "but you must go in by yourselves. Those are the regulations."

He took off their collars and leashes and pushed the door open for them, and Anatole stumbled after Captain Lark and Susannah into darkness and heard, with a sinking heart, the door close behind them.

As his eyes grew used to the dark, he saw they were standing in an enormous room, empty save for half a dozen torches that burned in sconces on the walls and threw long shadows across the rushes strewn over the stone floor.

"Nobody's here but us," said Anatole, relieved.

"Hush," warned Captain Lark. "Look where the shadows grow thickest, at the far end of the room. He's a bulldog today. That's unlucky for us."

Suddenly Anatole saw the Governor clearly: a giant bulldog sitting on an old blanket. The instant the boy saw him, the dog spoke.

"Come forward," he said in a slow rusty voice, "and tell your story."

His words called forth a small circle of light at the edge of the blanket, just big enough for one person to occupy. Anatole turned to Susannah, but in the darkness she was nearly invisible. The torchlight flickered and danced on Quicksilver's sides. The whole room seemed bent on doing them harm.

It was Captain Lark who stepped into the light first.

"Governor of the dogs, you see before you a poor

creature under enchantment. I was born Bartholomew Gosnold Lark, of Sweet Chalybeate, Virginia."

"Virginia," growled the dog softly. "Is that under the water or above it?"

"It is above the water at all times and under the stars at night and under the sun by day. I was the captain of the Morning Star, bound for Africa with a cargo of rum and gunpowder. We sailed out of Salem, Massachusetts, on June 23, 1850—"

"Why, Captain Lark," exclaimed Anatole, "that would make you over a hundred years old!"

"Enchantment," said the rabbit, "is a great preserver of youth."

"Be still!" barked the Governor. "Go on with your story."

"To put it plain, we were taken by pirates. My crew was murdered and I was given a choice: to join the pirates or be fed to the sharks. Against my will, I joined the pirates. A shipwreck landed me on this island, and a magician gave me this shape to punish me for stealing his gold."

Captain Lark wiped his forehead with the back of his paw and stepped back into the shadows. The bulldog remained silent for several minutes. Then he turned to Susannah.

"Tell me your story."

"I have no story yet," said Susannah. "I came here with this boy and a cat who is no longer among us. I have nobody else in the whole world."

Anatole did not wait for the Governor to demand his story.

"I am on my way to ask the King of the Grass—"

But he got no further, for at the words *King of the Grass*, the bulldog swelled to four times his size and rage shook his body like a storm.

"I condemn you to death! All of you! Let the swing be made ready at dawn!"

6.

The floor gave way beneath them and dropped them straight down into darkness. They landed on bare earth, shaken but unhurt.

"Where are we?" shouted Captain Lark.

"In the dungeon," hissed the Governor. Teeth bared, he peered down at them. Before any one of them could speak, he slammed the trap door shut and left them there. By the light of a tiny window high in the earthen wall, they looked at each other. Below the window, set with bars of polished bones, was the faint outline of a door that had neither latch nor lock, and a tangle of roots sealed it shut.

"Is this the end of everything?" asked Susannah. "This dark little room?"

"Stone walls do not a prison make," sang Captain Lark, but his good cheer sounded forced. "Climb on my shoulders, Anatole, and let's rattle the bars."

Anatole climbed up, but the window stayed out of reach, and Captain Lark refused to let Susannah climb on Anatole's shoulders for fear she would fall and break.

"Then it *is* the end," wailed Susannah.

"This may be the end or it may not be," said Captain Lark. "When the swing throws us up into the sky, we may simply find ourselves somewhere else. Then you can ask the first person we meet to point out the way to Mother Weather-sky's garden. If you need someone to protect you, I offer my services."

"Thank you," said Susannah.

"We would be very pleased to have you join us, Captain," said Anatole.

"What time do you think the dogs will come for us?" asked Susannah.

"Sunrise," the rabbit answered. "It was always sunrise when we sent our prisoners to walk the plank."

"To walk the plank?" repeated Susannah.

"To die," said Anatole.

"Oh, Captain Lark, how dreadful!"

"I'm very sorry, my lady," murmured the rabbit. "I won't speak of it again."

Suddenly a muffled voice rasped, "Move the stone and let me in!"

Quicksilver scooted away in terror. The stone on which he had been sitting shifted ever so little, and when Anatole lifted it up, a large rat put its head through the hole and blinked at them.

"Don't be afraid," whispered the rat. "Your friend the cat sent me to show you a way out of the dungeon. Follow me down the tunnel."

And the rat slipped out of sight. Quicksilver followed it, and Susannah, after peering carefully into the hole, climbed after Quicksilver.

"Come on, Captain Lark," called Anatole, easing himself in after Susannah.

From the mouth of the tunnel he heard Captain Lark's voice, trembling with disappointment.

"The door is too small for me. You go forward. I'll dig it wider and meet you later."

"You can't dig alone," said Anatole. He shouted for the others to help, and they all crawled back into the dungeon. The earth around the tunnel was soft. They dug fast and soon enlarged the entrance.

"This time let Captain Lark go first," said Anatole.

The rabbit lowered himself carefully into the tunnel until only his ears showed, their golden rings twinkling. Then he stopped.

"Keep going," urged Anatole. "What's the matter?"

"I'm stuck," grunted the rabbit. "The tunnel gets narrower here."

"Can't you back out the way you came?" asked Susannah. "We'll dig it wider."

"I can't go backward or forward," groaned Captain Lark.

They all began shouting at once, till a rap on the door under the window silenced them. Captain Lark, pushing and struggling, pulled himself back into the dungeon just as the roots that bound the door snapped apart and the loose earth trickled down the wall like tears.

The door broke open, and the Great Dane bounded into the room.

"Halt, or be torn to bits!" he barked.

He threw a circle of rope around them and pulled it tight, gathering them together like sheaves.

"Surely, you aren't going to execute us now," said Captain Lark. "Sunrise is the usual hour, I believe."

"For us there is no usual hour." The Great Dane smiled. "During the day you'd give our citizens a little amusement, but the Governor is eager to be rid of you. A noisier bunch he's never heard. And when he discovers this"—he pointed to the hole in the floor—"he'll thank his stars he didn't wait."

Anatole just had time to grab Quicksilver before the Great Dane herded them into the corridor. No lights glowed at the far end, and Anatole supposed that they had a long walk ahead of them, but soon the air grew cooler, and he glanced up and saw overhead the whole shimmering fabric of the stars.

"What beautiful lights live in the sky," said Susannah. They stepped outside. A spicy fragrance nearly took Anatole's breath away. Captain Lark wiggled his nose.

"It is the night-blooming cereus," he observed. "A great bush of it grew by the house in which I was born."

He spoke so calmly that Anatole asked, "Aren't you afraid?"

"Of high places, yes. When we ride up in the swing, please hold my paw."

A dead sycamore, bone white in the moonlight, rose over the crest of the hill to meet them. Anatole gave a gasp of relief. Instead of a place of execution, he saw a deserted playground. The swing was like the one in his backyard, though its ropes were longer and would travel farther.

"Lovely view," remarked the Great Dane. He untied the rope that bound them together. "We always give our prisoners time to admire the view."

Below them, in the valley of the dogs, moonlight touched every hummock of grass. A bird cried out in its sleep from a distant forest. Captain Lark drew a deep breath and said very quietly:

> "The earth is all before me: with a heart
> Joyous, nor scared at its own liberty,
> I look about, and should the guide I choose
> Be nothing better than a wandering cloud,
> I cannot miss my way."

"Are you a poet, sir?" asked the Great Dane.

"No, no. Once the tide brought me a book—"

"Time's up," snapped the Great Dane. "Into the swing."

"I have to face front or I shall be sick," said Captain Lark. He jumped up on the seat, grasped the ropes, and stood facing the place where, in a few hours, the sun would rise, though they would not be here to watch it. Nevertheless, he took care to keep a cheerful face, just as if he were starting out on a vacation.

"Susannah, you get in next, and then you, Anatole."

"Let's be a sandwich," said Anatole, "and Susannah can be the filling."

"I will hold Quicksilver," said Susannah.

They took their positions on the swing. Suddenly something sprang out of the darkness and landed on Anatole's shoulder. It was Plumpet.

"Don't say a word," she purred in his ear. "Didn't I promise to take care of you?"

The Great Dane, who did not notice Plumpet, sprang forward barking, and began to push the swing in long loping strokes, to and fro, to and fro. Now it was rising so swiftly that the dog could run under it. The air felt chillier. The swing was flying away from the earth. How faint his barking sounded! Glancing down, Anatole was astonished to find that the dog had shrunk to the size of a toadstool. On all sides, the stars drew near, like friendly lamps hanging from dark chains. They gave off a pleasant smell of hot wax.

"Hold my paw, please!"

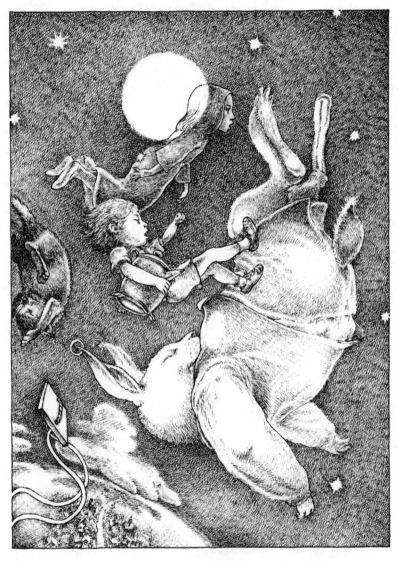

"THEN THE SWING GAVE A TREMENDOUS JERK, FLIPPED OVER,
AND THREW ITS PASSENGERS INTO THE SKY."

Anatole worked his hand up the ropes till he found the rabbit's paw. The rabbit's eyes were closed and his mouth was moving. Over the whistle of the wind, Anatole heard him shouting,

"Sunset and evening star,
    And one clear call for me!"

The ropes were lengthening like shadows at dusk, unleashed from an endlessly turning spool.

Anatole was filled with a terror so total that he nearly let go the ropes. Then the swing gave a tremendous jerk, flipped over, and threw its passengers into the sky.

7·

a, ha, ha!"

Anatole sat up. Who was laughing at him? The thick
fog rolling lazily around him opened to reveal Captain
Lark close by, sitting up and feeling himself for broken
bones. Then it closed like an eyelid, before blowing away
completely.

They had landed in a green field. Susannah was turning Quicksilver right side up. Plumpet's fur stood on end,
and she had fluffed her tail to three times its usual size.

"Ha, ha, ha!"

At the far end of the field grew an orchard, and in the middle of the orchard stood a white house, and on the veranda sat an old man and an old woman who leaned back in their rockers and roared with laughter.

"It is vexing to be laughed at in adversity," said Plumpet.

The old woman wiped her eyes and shouted, "BREAK-FAST!"

The old man watched them coming, then he rolled a bit of his beard into a thread, and called out, "Stop when the grass stops, and I'll throw you a line."

The grass ended at a broad band of glass, laid down in rainbow stripes like ribbon candy, which sloped away on either side of the house. Over this the old man tossed a line, and when they had all laid hold of it, he pulled them across as if he were reeling in a fish—and a good thing too, for the rainbow was so slick no one could keep a footing on it.

"Throw nothing away," said the old woman, taking the thread from him and tucking it into her pocket. "Save everything."

They were, thought Anatole, the oldest people he had ever seen. Their hands and faces were furrowed, like snow after children have played in it. The old woman wore a long dress of white wool, and the old man's suit was so white that his beard blended into his clothes; you could not tell where one started and the other left off. But even more curious, both the man and the woman wore roller skates instead of shoes, and the roller skates had wings. Wings the size of crocuses sprouted from the

"THEY WERE, THOUGHT ANATOLE, THE OLDEST PEOPLE HE HAD EVER SEEN."

rockers of the old couple's chairs, and a pair of wings no bigger than thimbles fluttered on each side of the old woman's mobcap.

"And what can we do for you?" she asked, wiping her eyes with the back of her hand.

"We would like breakfast," said Plumpet.

"Please," added Anatole.

"Have you lost your way?" asked the old man.

"Did you have a road?" asked the old woman.

"And did it say anything to you before it left?" asked the old man.

"And was it wearing roller skates?" asked the old woman eagerly.

Anatole shook his head, astonished.

"Now that's a pity." She sighed. "If it were wearing roller skates, it could easily find its way home."

"But roads don't wear roller skates," cried Captain Lark, who could hardly believe his ears.

The old woman nodded.

"Isn't that the truth now? I've seen roads out in the worst weather without their roller skates, and I tell them they'll never get anywhere in this world, they'll lose—"

"Friends, money, memory, everything. Ha, ha, ha!" shrieked the old man.

The old woman drew Anatole and Susannah toward her and said, "We're not laughing at you, my dears. It's the air up here that makes us so merry. If you stay long enough, it'll happen to you."

"I'm sorry we can't stay," said Anatole.

"Except for breakfast," added Plumpet.

"Breakfast!" the old woman called and clapped her hands. "Come here this instant!"

Out skated a little table, loaded with hotcakes and butter and three cruets of maple syrup. You could see that it had hurried. The wings on its legs were still pulsing.

"Naughty," scolded the old woman. "You've forgotten your chairs again."

Three big chairs and one small chair scooted out of the house and arranged themselves around the table. They scuffled for places next to the old woman, but it was wonderful to watch them settle their differences at last and wait politely to be sat on. It was even more wonderful to watch the small chair tread the air with its wings at the level of the table so Quicksilver could enjoy his breakfast.

"Don't they mind nicely, though?" The old man grinned. The dishes, fluttering their wings, passed themselves. The pot of cocoa obligingly poured itself into cups. A blue cup flew to Quicksilver, who dipped his spout into it like a beak and slurped joyfully. Susannah ate nothing; glass has no appetite. The others were so hungry that the platter went back twice for more hotcakes, round and white as buttered moons.

"Do you always wear roller skates?" inquired Plumpet. And forgetting her manners, she dipped her paw in the maple syrup. The old man and the old woman took no notice.

"Always," answered the old woman. "Our house sits

at the very top of the rainbow, and if we went about in shoes, we'd slide off. So roller skates with wings are the best way of getting around."

The old man, who was absorbed in counting first the dishes and then the guests, turned to Anatole and said, "Time to pay up. You ate three rounds of hotcakes and a pot of hot chocolate. Butter is free but syrup is extra."

"I'm sorry," said Anatole. "I didn't know we had to pay. We haven't any money."

"Neither have we," said the old woman, laughing. "Where on earth would we spend it?" She turned to Plumpet. "I suppose you know how to wash windows? You cats are great washers."

Plumpet sniffed at the nearest window and drew back in surprise.

"But your windows have no glass."

"Certainly not," exclaimed the old woman. "It's hard enough to keep my windows clean without having to keep the glass clean as well."

"Then how am I to wash them?"

"You must leap in and out of the windows and keep them distracted. They love to dream, and when they dream, they spin clouds. Woolgathering, I call it. Nothing beats leaping for cleaning windows."

"Do *you* leap in and out of the windows?" asked Plumpet. It struck her as a sight worth watching.

The old woman shook her head. "No, I send my sparrows to do it. They'll be glad of a day off."

Plumpet stretched herself and yawned; she did not

like heavy work. Nevertheless, she began to leap in and out of the windows as briskly as any sparrow while the others watched admiringly, and soon not a cloud could be seen. When she leaped through the last window, there was a burst of applause.

Anatole turned to the old man and the old woman. "Will you help us now?" asked Anatole. "We are going to Mother Weather-sky's garden—"

"I know where you're going," said the old woman. "My eyes see all roads, even invisible ones. Is it her golden key you want?"

"Yes, but the Keeper of the Roads said she wears it at her waist night and day," said Anatole.

"The Keeper of the Roads is mistaken," said the old woman. "He sleeps too much. He gets things muddled. The Magician hid the key. He never gave it to Mother Weather-sky."

"Oh," cried Susannah, "do you know where to find it?"

"No. Only the four great winds know that, for all the lost keys in the world pass through their hands at one time or another, and they know where everything is and where it belongs and who took it, and not even my sister Mother Weather-sky knows that much. So you must go to the four great winds and ask them."

"Are they good or bad?" inquired Plumpet.

The old woman stopped rocking her chair and considered the question carefully.

"Some call them thieves, others call them peddlers," she said at last.

"But if the four winds don't like you, nothing in the world can help you find the key," added the old man.

Suddenly the old woman jumped to her feet.

"My animals are running to their pastures!"

On the eastern horizon a great door, such as Anatole had seen on very large barns, began to take shape in the sky. Slowly it swung open, and out ran the animals, as pale as smoke and broken, as if they'd come from the bottom of a box of animal crackers. The zebra had only three paws, the elephant had lost its head, the tiger broke into four pieces before their eyes. In the next instant the zebra turned into a whale, the elephant dissolved into a thousand mice, the mice gathered themselves into a sheep. Anatole found he could not look at the same animal twice.

"Tomorrow I shall send one of my animals with you, and that will please the winds. They are very fond of my animals," said the old woman. "But tonight you shall all sleep in our house at the top of the rain."

And taking Susannah and Anatole by the hand, she led everyone up a back staircase to a loft filled with clouds. Anatole had only time to think, as he crawled into one of them, how odd it was to sleep in a bed that had no frame, in a house that had no roof. Or did the roof only go away at night?

"Downstairs it was morning. How is it I can see the stars?" he asked her.

The old woman laughed.

"This is where we keep the night. We have rooms and

rooms of it, and every evening we let it out and every morning it comes back."

When Anatole felt Plumpet curling at his feet, he closed his eyes and did not open them till he heard the old woman calling him for breakfast.

After they had eaten, the old woman gathered Anatole and his friends close to her as if she were going to tell them a story.

"Are you ready to meet the four winds?" she asked.

"What if they won't see us?" asked Captain Lark.

"They'll see you," said the old woman. "They're my husband's brothers, and they never turn away our friends."

And pulling a handful of wool from her apron pocket, she tossed it and turned it between her palms and nudged it here and tugged it there till she had stretched it into a huge fish. Its skin was so thin that you could see right into its empty heart.

"That's a rare one," observed Captain Lark. "It has wings instead of fins."

"I'm glad you like it," said the old woman. "I meant to make a bird."

With one finger she outlined a door on the fish's scales and opened it.

"Hurry inside," she urged, "before it changes into something else. Nothing I make lasts very long, you know."

When they had taken their places, she closed the door and smoothed the scales back into place and called the old man. He was leading the animals back to the great door. Spying the fish, he laughed and puffed up his cheeks and blew.

Wheee! The grass laid itself flat as a cat's ears, and the fish swam into the air like a kite. Through its pale skin, Anatole watched the clouds that roared past with the faces of horsemen, riding the old man's breath. They let loose such a shouting and crying that the travelers in the fish were obliged to hold their ears, except Quicksilver, who couldn't find his.

8.

They came to rest on an island in the middle of a lake, close by a small house, which was cobbled with seashells from top to bottom. The shutters were thrown open, and there was an awful row going on inside. Before Anatole could find the door in its side, the fish flew straight up to the roof and dived down the chimney and landed softly in the middle of an enormous room.

A piano whistled past them. Books circled the room like lost birds. Gravestones, steeples, lanterns, armchairs, and fishnets flew over the heads of four men whose white hair streamed around them as they stood in the four corners of the room and shouted. You could tell who was the North Wind, for he was the biggest and strongest; and you could tell the East Wind, for he was the youngest and smallest; and you could tell the South Wind, who was very handsome and looked as if fighting really did not agree with him at all. That left only one more, a rather mysterious figure dressed entirely in black, who Anatole concluded was certainly the West Wind—since the others had been accounted for.

"The cupboard belongs to me! I found it!" shrieked the East Wind.

"Then give me back my suitcase," the West Wind hissed.

A suitcase sailed across the room. The West Wind snatched it out of the air and inspected it.

"You've torn the hinges!"

"You tore them yourself!"

Suddenly the four winds caught sight of the fish.

"Brothers," shouted the South Wind, "our sister has sent us a present."

They all wanted to have it, of course, and they began tumbling the fish to and fro about the room. Hearing shrieks from inside, they turned it upside down and shook it till the passengers came rattling out like peas in a shooter, and then the four winds grew still with astonishment. In all their travels they had never seen a company exactly like this one. The East Wind pulled Captain Lark's ears, the South Wind picked up Anatole and

Quicksilver and juggled with them, the West Wind balanced Plumpet on his thumb, and the North Wind set Susannah gently on his palm and brought her close to his great eyes, for he was very shortsighted.

"This creature's made of living glass," said the North Wind, raising Susannah like a goblet, "so we mustn't throw her about. Be careful with the others as well, brothers. They, too, may be alive."

At once the South Wind set Anatole and Quicksilver on the floor, and the East Wind stood Captain Lark beside Anatole, and the West Wind arranged Plumpet between them, as if he were setting up pieces for a game of chess.

"You should have told us you were alive," scolded the North Wind, and he shook his finger at Susannah, who was huddled in the palm of his hand. "Those who ride our breath seldom arrive with any of their own. I can see that our sister sent you. Why?"

Anatole, still reeling, stepped forward, and the four brothers turned their ears toward him, so that they would not miss a word. Then he explained why he had left home and how he had met Susannah and Captain Lark and how they escaped from the dogs and how he meant to find the key and free the King of the Grass, unless Mother Weather-sky found it first, only he didn't know where to look for it. When he had finished, the North Wind spoke.

"You're a plucky fellow, and I like plucky fellows. I know where the key is. Maybe you're the lad that's to have had it?"

Anatole did not know what to say to this, but the North Wind did not wait for an answer.

"Not even my brothers know where the key is. And all sorts of folks come to me asking for it. They've heard of a golden castle, you know, and they want to get rich. Do you want to get rich?"

"I want my grandmother to get well."

"Well, you're the right one," said the North Wind. "The golden castle was nothing but one of the Magician's illusions. However, I never give anything away, not even to heroes. It's bad for business. What have you got to trade?"

"What do you want?" asked Anatole.

"Look around. What do I need?"

Anatole looked around. So did Plumpet and Captain Lark and Susannah, and even Quicksilver turned slowly around, so that the wealth of the winds was reflected in his bright side. It seemed to Anatole that the winds needed nothing, except perhaps a housekeeper to tidy their belongings.

"You have everything," said Susannah.

"Never mind that. What can you offer me?" asked the North Wind.

Susannah's whistle began to glow, and Anatole hastily stepped in front of her, for fear the North Wind would ask for it. Then he put his hand into his left pocket, hoping to find his harmonica, but to his great disappointment he found nothing but a yellow card.

The North Wind drew forward eagerly.

"What's that?"

"That's my YMCA card."

"What does the writing on it say?" demanded the North Wind.

"It says I belong to the YMCA."

"And what is the YMCA?"

"It's the place where I go swimming with my friends on Saturday mornings."

"And of what use is this card?"

"I show it to the lady at the door and she lets me in."

"Glory and onions!" shouted the North Wind. "All my life I've wanted people to let me in. They lock their doors. They button up. They won't listen. Did you say she'll have to let me in?"

Anatole read the card once more. It said nothing about not admitting the wind.

"If you show this card, she'll let you in."

"It's a trade!" The North Wind blew the card into the air, caught it between his teeth, rolled it up, and tucked it into his ear, which looked as if it were smoking.

"And now I'll tell you all I know about the key. It's hidden in Mother Weather-sky's garden, and I can take you there. But you must wait till I load my pack and put on my skis."

The South Wind and the East Wind were riding the fish around the room, while the West Wind ran after them, clamoring for his turn and shouting that the fish was growing fainter and fainter and would soon disappear. But the North Wind fetched a large leather bag from a hook on the wall and strode around stuffing various articles into it, including the West Wind's suitcase. He never liked to keep things long anyway; it was the getting and the getting rid of them that pleased him most. Next the North Wind put on his cape and took down his skis from their rack over the door and strapped them on his feet.

"Time to go," he said. "Jump on my pack."

"We'll be blown away," protested Susannah.

"Hold fast to my hair, then," said the North Wind. "I shall not feel it."

First Anatole climbed up, holding Quicksilver. Then Susannah got behind him with Plumpet in her arms. And last of all was Captain Lark, because he was the tallest and his arms reached around everyone else and kept them in place like the sides of a ship. The North Wind opened the door, took a deep breath, and pushed off.

What a fine figure he made, skiing down currents of air and shouting to himself.

"Look down," he called over his shoulder. "Once upon a time those trees were towers and cloud-capped palaces. On still days, when I'm not around, you can hear bells ringing in the ground."

"Bells ringing in the ground?" repeated Anatole.

"The Magician couldn't change them, so he buried them. Below us is Mother Weather-sky's garden. Jump off now."

But his passengers clung to his hair like burrs.

"WHAT A FINE FIGURE HE MADE, SKIING DOWN CURRENTS OF AIR
AND SHOUTING TO HIMSELF."

"Jump off! Or I'll shake you off."

And since they would not let go, the North Wind arched his back and sent them flying into a holly bush. They had hardly landed when lightning exploded all around them, bushes were ripped from the earth and hurled into the sky, branches rushed through the air like bits of paper, and a huge tree lurched in front of them and fell, screeching like an animal. The storm did not touch the holly bush where they lay, but the forest around them was being laid waste. A thunderous baying of dogs made Anatole glance up in terror. Through the leaves of the holly bush, he saw a pack of dogs running through the air overhead, and he recognized them as those dogs that had taken them prisoners. On the back of the Great Dane rode an old woman in a green cloak, and she was braiding whips of lightning and tossing them into the trees. The dogs sank lower and lower and raced yapping around the holly bush.

And then, just as suddenly, the air was so still that Anatole could hear the pounding of his heart. Cautiously, he peeped out and what he saw in that deep silence astonished him. The broken trees were mending themselves, standing up and putting forth new leaves and new boughs. Moss and partridge berries and wild mint were covering the forest floor once again.

"Who saved us?" whispered Susannah.

In the silence that followed, a small voice said, "I did. Though I am smaller than Mother Weather-sky, my spells are stronger."

"Who are you? Where are you?" cried Anatole, glancing around but seeing nobody.

"Look down," murmured the voice. "I'm resting on your shoe. Just a moment, I'm changing. Now you'll see me."

Across his left sneaker a tenuous shape appeared, a small green flame that grew brighter and brighter but gave off neither heat nor smoke. Anatole stooped and put out his hand, and a chameleon glided over his wrist and arranged itself on his palm.

"It's always hard for me to make myself different from what keeps me. Can you see me now?"

"Oh, yes!" everyone exclaimed. They could not take their eyes off the tiny lizard. It had silver claws and iridescent skin, and when Anatole lifted it for the others to examine, it turned its head this way and that and blinked its ruby eyes at them and darted its tiny blue tongue, fiery and forked, like a bolt of lightning.

"How lovely you are," exclaimed Susannah. "But how do you know Mother Weather-sky?"

"I can't tell you that," answered the chameleon. "I can only show you the road to her house."

"If your spells are stronger than hers, won't you make us good and wise and strong?" pleaded Anatole. He was certain the chameleon could make them invincible if it wanted to.

"What gifts can I give you that you haven't already got?" asked the chameleon softly. "Haven't you escaped the dogs and traveled on the wind? Haven't you survived Mother Weather-sky's storms and darknesses?"

This was true. But just then it did not seem enough.

"To reach Mother Weather-sky's house," continued the chameleon, "you must stop at her sister's."

"We've already met her sister," said Plumpet.

"You met her older sister. You haven't met her younger sister. The door to her house lies in the stream. You must go back the way you came."

Anatole set the chameleon down. Feeling solid ground under its feet, it slipped away into the darkness, but its skin gave off a trail of sparks, which flared up for an instant—long enough to light the path—and then died away and flared up again farther on. The travelers followed till the earth grew soft underfoot and the rushing and tumbling of water sounded close by.

"Stop," cautioned the chameleon. "I don't want you to fall into the stream."

"What must we do now?" asked Plumpet, who disliked getting wet paws under any circumstances; she always caught cold afterward.

"You must wait for the full moon," answered the chameleon.

"Heavens," exclaimed Captain Lark, "we may be stranded here for a month."

Nevertheless, he sat down between Anatole and Susannah on the banks of the stream. Susannah was nearly invisible, like a window in a dark house, and Quicksilver was all darkness, but the others could hear him stamping happily in the mud. Plumpet alone waited with grace and goodwill. Years of waiting at mouseholes had given her great patience.

Suddenly Susannah glowed with a lacy radiance; her glass body held the silvery branches of trees. Anatole scanned the sky for a full moon.

"You're looking in the wrong place," said the chameleon. "Go down."

They looked down. The full moon shone clear and pale in the water.

"I see a door," said Susannah.

"That's not a door," Anatole corrected her. "That's the moon's reflection." But the moment he said it, he was not so sure. Behind the gauzy circle on the water he saw a long stairway that led down into the stream, and he was quick to point it out to the others.

"I suppose I must take the plunge," said Plumpet with a sigh.

"I can't swim a stroke," said Captain Lark.

"That's odd for a pirate," observed Anatole.

"It is, isn't it? But it's so."

"I'm afraid I shall simply sink," said Susannah.

"Can none of us swim?" asked Captain Lark. "We need someone who can save us. Anatole, can you save us?"

"I can swim," said Anatole, "but I can't save anyone. I'm still in the beginner's class."

"You can swim," said the cat. "I vote Anatole go first."

"And I'll go next," volunteered Susannah, "and I shall hold your paw, Captain Lark, if you'd like me to."

The cat, the rabbit, the glass girl, and the coffeepot lined up on the bank. Anatole took a deep breath and held his nose and jumped—he had not yet learned how to dive—into the white circle.

9·

The water was so cold that it took Anatole's breath away. The next instant he got it back again, and he found himself on the stairway he had seen from the shore. He was quite dry, even his clothes, which smelled as fresh and clean as on the day his mother had bought them. Through the skin of water over his head, he saw his friends peering anxiously down at him, and he waved encouragingly.

"Come in! It's all right!" he shouted. But he could tell from their faces that they didn't hear him. He waved once more, then turned and started down the stairs. The darkness would have frightened him if the stairs had not reminded him of the ones that led to the fruit cellar in his grandmother's house.

"I wonder if there'll be old fruit jars and canned pears and boxes of Christmas ornaments," he said to himself. He listened for an echo but heard none, and it relieved him to know that the passage was not very large and that he was not likely to meet anyone in it. The stairs turned and ended abruptly at a wooden door, under which a yellow light shone on the stone landing. Anatole knocked twice. Nobody opened the door.

"Perhaps she's asleep," he said, and he lifted the latch and, finding it unlocked, went in.

The room into which he stepped was not at all like his grandmother's cellar but more like his mother's sewing room. A long worktable in the middle of the room was heaped with mending, and the young woman seated there was sorting, just as his mother did, and talking to herself.

"This is usable. This can be saved. But this is worn clean through. This I can use for patching. This I can piece together. But nothing can be done with this one— it's all holes. Well, nothing I mend lasts forever."

She did not look like his mother. She wore a brown robe made of dead leaves stitched close together, one on the other, and at first glance, she seemed to be wearing scales. Her hair was tucked out of sight under a lace scarf, cut and stitched from leaves that had been eaten away by insects so that only the veins remained. And now he noticed she was not sorting old clothes. Through her hands passed skins, feathers, claws, horns, antlers, fins, bones. They littered the floor. They covered the table. She ran her fingers over them, rubbed them, and held them up to the lamp. The lamp made Anatole shudder. Three serpents, twisted into a knot, hung from the ceiling, and the mouth of each serpent held a candle.

"A little more light over here, please," ordered the lady, and the snakes shifted obligingly, and lit up, briefly, a huge fireplace on the far side of the room, where a large soup pot hung, not over the fire but over a phosphorescent log, such as one occasionally finds in very damp forests.

"No, over here," urged the lady, and again the snakes shifted. This time the light from their candles fell directly on her hands and their strange business, but it also caught the dark corners of the room. And now Anatole gave a little cry of surprise—he had thought the room empty. He saw it was full of creatures kneeling on the floor and perched on the rafters overhead. There were otters, shrikes, stoats, deer, hawks, owls, woodchucks, crows, mice, and moles; there were creatures that hunt and creatures that are hunted, and they were all waiting together quietly at the edge of the light. Some had lost a wing or a foot, others had not so much as a leg to stand on, a few were torn beyond recognition. Those that had heads to turn turned them toward Anatole.

Suddenly the door sprang open, and Susannah, Captain Lark, Plumpet, and Quicksilver tumbled noisily into the room.

"...THE LIGHT FROM THEIR CANDLES FELL DIRECTLY ON HER HANDS
AND THEIR STRANGE BUSINESS..."

The Mender started from her chair, and Anatole noticed what an elegant chair it was, carved with shapes of the very animals that hovered in the darkness at her feet.

"Come here, please," she commanded, "one at a time. My sight has grown bad from working in the dark. But at close range, I can see everything."

Her fingers were darning a crow's wing as she spoke, and they never missed a stitch. Anatole came forward, and she brought her pale-blue eyes close to his green ones. Her face was as smooth and white as a mushroom.

"So my chameleon found you, after all," she said.

"We came for—" began Anatole, in a quavering voice, but she stopped him.

"I know what you came for," said the Mender. She nodded at the cat. "Next!"

Plumpet, who had grown faint in the presence of so many incautious moles and mice, crept to the Mender's feet and crouched there. The Mender stroked her fur appraisingly.

"You don't need mending," she said. "Your coat is in excellent repair. Next!"

At the sight of Quicksilver rolling across the floor, the Mender laughed.

"Little pot," she said, "you've nothing to fear from me. Go make friends with my big iron kettle in the fireplace. Oh, the stories it could tell you! Next!"

Captain Lark thumped forward, his wooden leg clattering on the stone floor. The Mender shook her head at him.

"I only mend creatures who are what they always

were. You're an enchanted being. Now, if you were a real rabbit—"

"No, thank you," said Captain Lark hastily, and he hurried to take his place next to Anatole, for fear the Mender might magic him into a real rabbit.

"Next!"

When Susannah stepped out, the light from the serpents set her golden whistle sparkling. The Mender looked long and hard at her.

"My servant the adder told me about you," she said. "She tells me what treasures lie under the earth."

"Where is the adder?" asked Anatole. He remembered how he discovered Susannah by tossing a stone at just such a snake.

"She's gone to Mother Weather-sky's house," said the Mender. "So you want to go there, too, do you?"

"The chameleon said you could show us the way," said Anatole.

"I can show you the way," said the Mender, "but I've got to find it first. Help me clean up the workroom. You could lose your own name in this mess."

And she patted Susannah on the shoulder, for the glass girl had already found the broom and was sweeping the floor. Everyone set about straightening, picking up, and putting away. The room reminded Anatole of a barbershop; feathers and fur lay in little piles underfoot, like hair clippings. In the dark corners, the animals stirred; there was a flutter of broken wings, a light shifting of broken bodies.

"That'll do," said the Mender. "Now come to my worktable, so I can see you under the light."

Susannah stood the broom in the corner, where she had found it. Plumpet picked a feather from her claws, and they joined Anatole and Captain Lark and Quicksilver around the Mender's marvelous chair. She put her arms around them, as if she intended to mend them, too.

"Tonight you shall sleep here, and tomorrow you shall find yourself in Mother Weather-sky's garden. My meals are informal; pick what you would like from my chair."

At these words, the ornaments on the chair woke up, and the carved animals slipped out of sight, leaving behind the branches of the remarkable tree on which they had been perched. Oranges, grapes, melons, pears, peaches, apples, and pomegranates grew there, ripened to perfection. Anatole ate two apples and three pears and was sure he had never tasted better. Plumpet, who generally did not touch fruit, batted a peach with her paw and to her delight it divided itself into two saucers of cream.

When they had eaten all they wished, the chair went back to sleep again; the carved animals returned to their branches, which grew still and dark and hard once more, and the chair behaved like any chair in the ordinary world.

The Mender pointed to a wall in which could be seen a pair of closed shutters.

"From this window I cast my nets each evening and gather what needs to be mended. Tonight while you are sleeping, I will throw my nets over you. Whatever they touch travels in its sleep. You will wake up in Mother Weather-sky's house."

"Do the nets ever make mistakes?" asked Captain Lark.

The Mender shook her head.

"The way to Mother Weather-sky's house is so cleverly hidden that no one can possibly find it with his eyes open."

"But when we arrive," said Anatole, "how can we find the key?"

The Mender smiled.

"You must see to that yourself. I will give you the one other thing that's needed to free the King of the Grass. But mind Mother Weather-sky doesn't take it from you, or you are lost."

She reached under her apron and brought forth a small brown book. The leather cover was so plain and so tattered that it scarcely looked worth the trouble of opening it.

"This is the *Red Calfskin Book of Magic* that belonged to the Magician, who enchanted this island."

Anatole gasped; the others stretched forth their hands timidly to touch it.

"But the Keeper of the Roads said it was lost!" exclaimed the boy.

"Nothing is lost forever," said the Mender. "Everything under the earth and in the sea comes back to me, one way or another. This book was a long time in coming. It has traveled in the guts of a fish, in the body of a bird, in the fourth chamber of an elk's stomach. It has given its leaves for the nests of ravens. It has fed wasps, it has shaped cocoons. It is a much better book than when it was first made, for it was a proud thing then, and now it's part book and part animal. It feels pain, it is wary, and it is mortal. You'll find the spell you need on the last page, the only page that is left."

She handed the book to Anatole, who opened it at once.

"The last page is empty!" he exclaimed.

"No, it's not. The words of the spell are there. But they are invisible."

"Then how am I to read them?" demanded Anatole.

"I am sorry to tell you that only one living soul can read those words," answered the Mender, "and he is not very friendly. The wild boar who lives in Mother Weather-sky's garden can read all languages, even the invisible ones. But capturing him will be very dangerous. Above all, remember to take nothing from Mother Weather-sky's garden."

"Of course we won't," said Captain Lark.

"Not a thing," agreed Plumpet.

"If you do, you will be in Mother Weather-sky's power, and she will most certainly destroy you."

The Mender waited till Anatole had tucked the magic book into his back pocket. Then she rose and deftly plucked a snake out of her lamp and coiled it around her arm.

"Come. I'll show you to your room."

The travelers followed her into a small room, even darker than the first one but less crowded, for it had no worktable and no fireplace, and nothing on the floor except half a dozen wings scattered about like rugs. They shimmered gold and silver, as if the feathers had been worked in metal.

"Did angels leave these?" whispered Anatole.

"Not angels," replied the Mender. "Basilisks and dragons. Their wings are so warm you will not need a cover."

Anatole sank sleepily into the nearest wing, and Plumpet curled herself at his feet, for she had promised to take care of him and she always kept her promises. It seemed to the boy that he heard bells ringing far under the earth and that the bells had voices, deep and muffled:

> "Three women sailed out of the watery dark,
> and who do you think they be?
> The Mender, the Maker, the Bender-and-Breaker,
> Wise women, all three!"

The harmonica in his pocket hummed quick and high, which frightened Anatole very much, till he remembered the Roadkeeper's words: "Don't be afraid. The island is full of noises. Sometimes a thousand twangling instruments will hum about your ears, and sometimes voices. And if you've waked after a long sleep, they'll make you sleep again."

The music ceased as suddenly as it had started, and the last voice he heard belonged to Plumpet, who declared herself so moved by the spectacle of the wounded creatures in the workshop that she would never go hunting again—at least not till the next full moon.

10.

The next morning the Mender and her creatures were nowhere to be seen, and the travelers awoke to find themselves surrounded by a queer throng of folk who stood perfectly still with their feet in the sand and their eyes raised to heaven, as if they were praying for deliverance. Many of the women wore wings like angels, though they had caps instead of haloes, and they were waving flags, from which the colors had long been weathered away, so that you could not tell what countries they came from. The men wore periwigs or stovepipe hats or sailor suits; a few were dressed as Indian chieftains. The ladies who did not look like angels wore long gowns and bonnets. Scattered among this solemn crowd were eagles, lions, unicorns, mermaids, and a large robust figure who might have been King of the Sea, for he held a trident and wore a crown, both badly in need of paint. And nearly everyone carried banners inscribed with such names as *Constitution* or *Glory of the Sea* or *Clara Belle* or *Polar Star* or *Dashing Wave*.

Anatole felt anxiously in his pocket for the magician's book. Yes, it was quite safe.

"What funny names these people have," whispered Susannah. "They don't seem to notice us at all. I believe we can walk right past them."

"Bless me, they're figureheads," exclaimed Captain Lark. "Many's the time I've admired such things on the prows of passing ships. But how odd to find them all heaped together in a field."

A narrow flagstone path wound through the crowd of figureheads in Mother Weather-sky's garden. The garden was laid out in beds, but no flowers grew in them. Sextants and compasses glittered in one, broken crockery shone in another, chests empty of treasure—their lids open or gone entirely—lay in a third. The path led past a jumble of weathervanes—roosters and archers and fish and horses—that had long ago lost their sense of direction; motionless, they pointed to the earth.

Then the path turned abruptly. At last, and to Anatole's great delight, it entered a bed of toys. Model ships, steam engines, trucks, cars, cradles, puppets, dolls, like the stockroom of the biggest toy store in the world, except that everything was broken, everything had been battered by the sea. Anatole paused to finger a small ship that had lost its sails. Its ivory hull felt smooth as butter, and its brass spars shone.

"Do you think a sailor made this for his child back home?" he asked Captain Lark. But the rabbit only shook his head.

"Remember what the Mender told us," he warned. "Take nothing from the garden."

Anatole did not mean to take the ship, only to hold it. But the instant he picked it up, he felt a blow on his head that knocked him to the ground. He was back on his feet at once, and again something struck him, this time on the shoulder. He looked up. A stick twice the size of his baseball bat at home was dancing over his head. Now it pummeled Captain Lark on the back, and now it darted after Plumpet and nipped her tail, so that she mewed dreadfully. Fortunately it did not touch Susannah.

"Run!" the glass girl screamed.

They ran down the path, the stick bobbing after them, as if it rode an invisible wave. In their haste to escape, nobody noticed that the end of the path was near and that it led straight into the side of a broken ship, which somebody had patched up to make a house. In the doorway stood a little woman wrapped in a green cape, like an ear of corn, and she was puffing on a pipe. She blew out a great cloud of smoke and said, "Stick, lay off."

The stick stopped in mid-blow and leaped obediently into her hand. Anatole glanced round to see who had saved them.

"Don't move," said the woman. "My ash stick can split a rock if it chooses."

"Who are you?" cried Susannah.

"I am Mother Weather-sky," came the reply.

Anatole stared at her. She was without doubt the same woman he had seen riding the dogs and throwing lightning bolts during the storm. But by the calm light of a windless day how small she looked! She might have been one of the plaster dwarves at the back of his grandmother's garden. Her cape needed mending, her boots were split at the toes, and her blue apron, faded almost to gray, was smudged with ashes. Her hair was tangled with burrs and branches and—could it be? A sparrow had actually built its nest and was sitting on top of its eggs, fast asleep, just over her left ear.

"I'm not afraid of you," said Anatole. "You aren't much taller than my cat."

"Smaller is stronger," said Mother Weather-sky, and she stalked over to Plumpet and shook the ashes from her pipe over the cat's ears and tail.

What happened next made Anatole regret his words. Plumpet's honey-warm fur grew hard and bright, her whiskers began to shimmer, her claws shone, and where the lively cat had crouched a moment before he saw a cat of pure gold.

"She shall be my bench," said Mother Weather-sky,

"THE STICK STOPPED IN MID-BLOW AND LEAPED OBEDIENTLY INTO HER
HAND."

puffing on her pipe. Then she walked from Anatole to Susannah to Captain Lark, her wicked green eyes peering at each of them in turn. Before Anatole could stop her, she took the pipe from her mouth once more and threw a shower of ashes over Captain Lark. Without a sound he curled up like a leaf in a bonfire, smooth and still, stretched in a golden sleep.

"A very serviceable table," said Mother Weather-sky. Then she turned to Quicksilver.

"Down the path that branches to the right, you will find a well. Take the rope and climb down and fetch my water. Do not take the other path or things will go badly for you."

The coffeepot marched away sorrowfully, dragging its silver feet.

Mother Weather-sky grabbed Susannah by the wrist and asked, "Can you cook? If you can cook, I shall keep you for a little while longer before I break you to bits and take that whistle."

Susannah shrank behind Anatole, but Mother Weather-sky yanked her out and pushed her toward the open door, which was so low that the girl had to crawl through it on her hands and knees.

"My kitchen lies to the back," called Mother Weather-sky after her. "I like tea with my meals and I'm very fond of currants."

Susannah disappeared into Mother Weather-sky's house. It had not a single window; even the portholes were sealed up. Mother Weather-sky folded her arms and cocked her head at Anatole.

"My vegetable garden wants weeding. I am fond of vegetables, but where I walk weeds spring up. The center path will lead you to the vegetable plot. Pull every weed by sundown or I shall change you into a turnip and eat you for supper."

Anatole did not wait to be told twice. He ran down the path and almost immediately found the vegetable garden. It was so overgrown with burdock and thistles that ten men could not have cleared it in a week, and he knew he could never clear it in a day, for he had no spade and no rake, nothing but his bare hands.

But even worse than the weeds were the stones. He kept stubbing his toes on them. Soon he was so weary that he had to sit down, and when he remembered Susannah in that dark little house, Plumpet and Captain Lark changed into furniture, and his own fate if he didn't finish, he burst into tears.

Something splashed, not far from where he sat. He looked around startled and was very surprised to discover among the weeds a clear pool, perfectly round, just to his left. He ran to it eagerly and leaned over the rim to drink and saw, at the same moment, two golden fish—one large, one small—gliding slowly through the water, their tails fanning gently back and forth. Then he spied something else gleaming in the darkness at the bottom of the pool, and he drew in his breath and gave a cry of delight.

It was the golden key.

Before he could reach for it, a blossom sailed down

from the tree overhead and glided to the water. The touch of the water turned the blossom to stone and it started to sink. But now a strange thing happened. The water, so still and clear, began to churn and stir itself, foaming and frothing, until at last the waves leaped up like hands and flung the stone flower out of the water.

Anatole jumped back in a hurry.

"It's a good thing I didn't drink from that pool."

A snorting and crashing among the trees at the far side of the pool made him freeze in his tracks. Something was charging toward him, heaving dirt into the air as it came. There flashed across his mind his mother's lullaby about the boy who played the harmonica so well that all the animals lay down around him, even the fiercer kinds, and in desperation he felt for his harmonica in his back pocket, pulled it out, and tried to play his old standby, "Yankee Doodle." To his surprise it began to play his mother's lullaby instead:

> "Everything that heard him play,
>   even the billows of the sea,
> hung their heads and then lay by."

The crashing and snorting among the trees stopped, and a husky voice supplied the rest of the words:

> "In sweet music is such art,
>   killing care and grief of heart,
> fall asleep or hearing, die."

Into the sunlight trotted a wild boar. It was as big as a horse, and its tusks curled over its snout like two nicely matched scythes. Humming to itself, it sat down beside Anatole and then it said, "Leave off and catch your breath."

"Aren't you going to run me through?" quavered Anatole, who was almost too frightened to speak.

"No sense in running you through," replied the boar. "I've few enough folk as it is. What brings you to this dreadful place?"

So Anatole told the boar how he and his friends had fallen into Mother Weather-sky's power and he had little hope they would ever get home again. And he added that he wanted to free the King of the Grass, but he did not mention the Magician's book. The boar listened gravely.

"I am well acquainted with the King of the Grass. I was his gardener."

"Then you know where to find him?" asked Anatole eagerly.

"No. I won't see him till I carry five and sink alive. That's part of the spell. What do you think it means? Five of what? Sink into what? And where's the lost key to be found?"

"The key is in the pool," Anatole exclaimed, pointing, "but if you touch the water, you'll turn to stone."

The boar squinted into the water. "As I live and breathe! Now if we only had the lost book of spells, we'd go straight to the door."

"Could you read the lost book of spells?" asked Anatole.

"HUMMING TO ITSELF, IT SAT DOWN BESIDE ANATOLE..."

"I can read all languages," said the boar, "even the invisible ones."

Hearing this, Anatole brought the book from his pocket and handed it to the boar, who sniffed it all over and raised his head slowly so that his tiny eyes met Anatole's.

"How did you come by this?"

"The Mender gave it to me."

"Wonderful!" exclaimed the boar. "Hey, my dears"— he called out to the two fish, who flamed through the dark water—"bring us the key, won't you? You know I can't reach it myself."

The biggest fish leaped out of the water, spat the key out into Anatole's pocket, turned a somersault, and disappeared again into the depths.

"That's a good fellow," said the boar. "Now let's see what the book advises."

He opened it to the last and only page. When the light struck it, the letters began to fade in, like invisible ink before a candle. Anatole could make nothing of the words, but the boar read in a low voice:

"One for the rook, one for the crow,
one to die, and one to grow."

And now before Anatole's eyes, the strange words shifted and slowly changed themselves into the words he knew. In the R of rook crouched a rabbit, in the C of crow dozed a cat, in the G of grow stood a girl. The D of die opened up into a door, through which something had just passed, for you could see part of its shadow, but you could not tell what it was.

The boar continued:

"When bells ring clear,
summer is near."

At these words the page faded into smoke and the cover of the book crumpled into a handful of dry leaves.

"Well, well," said the boar, brushing off his paws. "I've come to the end of the spell. Do you hear the bells ringing clear?"

Anatole heard nothing. Then it seemed to him he did hear something—was it the wind? No, it was the bells, some deep and sonorous as church bells, some high and brilliant as chimes. The boar pricked up his ears.

"They're ringing from over that way," said Anatole, pointing east.

"Let's follow them," said the boar, and he trotted away so briskly that Anatole had to run to keep up with him.

I I .

he bells led the boy and the boar into a eu-
calyptus grove so dense that even the path could not find
its way and simply disappeared under broken branches.
The hulls of ships, half sunk in the mud, jutted through
the underbrush. Enormous vines spread like nets at their
feet, and when Anatole heard something crackling in the
bushes, he called out, "Is there another boar in the forest?" just as the boar exclaimed, "I shall charge at it,
whatever it is," and the branches burst apart and out tumbled Susannah, Captain Lark, Plumpet, and Quicksilver.

There were shouts of astonishment and cries of joy.

"How did you escape?" demanded Anatole, who could hardly believe his eyes.

"Quicksilver saved us," said Captain Lark. "When he brought the water from Mother Weather-sky's well, he saw her sprinkle it on a stone. The stone turned into a quail, which she ordered Susannah to cook for supper. So he took some of the water and sprinkled us back to life again."

"And then I crept through the kitchen door and found Susannah," added Plumpet.

"And I jumped out and we ran away." Susannah laughed, clapping her hands till they rang like crystal.

Suddenly she caught sight of the boar, who had concealed himself in the foliage and now came forward to introduce himself. She gave a little shriek, and the others spun around in a panic.

"Don't be afraid," said Anatole. "This is my friend, Mr.—Mr.—"

"Toby," said the boar. "The name's Toby."

"This is Toby," continued Anatole, "and he has gotten us the golden key and he has read the spell in the Magician's book, and we were following the bells through the forest and looking for the golden tree."

"Bells?" inquired Plumpet.

"Let's listen again for the bells," said Toby. "I am sure they will lead us to the King of the Grass."

They stood still and listened. The bells had stopped ringing, but another noise could be heard very distinctly, a thwack, thwack, which came from the direction of Mother Weather-sky's house.

"Somebody's chopping down trees," said Plumpet.

Toby let out a howl.

"She's found us," he bellowed. "That's her stick we hear, and it's marching through the forest after us. We must run for our lives."

"But where can we go?" wailed Susannah.

"To the river at the back of Mother Weather-sky's garden," answered Toby. "She can't swim. Climb on my back. I can push aside the branches with my tusks."

There was a mad scramble for places. They could hear the stick coming closer—thwack, thwack—and though Toby was running as fast as he could, the stick was running faster. Sitting behind Captain Lark, in the last place, Anatole looked back and saw the stick springing among the trees. And riding on the stick was Mother Weather-sky herself.

"She's right behind us!" shouted Anatole. "Hurry!"

Susannah began to laugh.

"The river! I see the river! We're saved!"

Toby rushed toward it and plunged down an embankment so steep that he nearly pitched his passengers over his head. Mother Weather-sky, whipping her stick, was bounding right after them. When Anatole looked back once more, her hand brushed his arm, and it felt cold as snow, just as Toby reached the water and waded in.

Behind them, Mother Weather-sky was dancing on the muddy banks and shouting, "May you turn into stones and sink! May the fish swallow you! May you never find your way home!"

"She's casting a spell on us," yowled Plumpet.

"No, she's not," said Toby. "She has no power over the river."

The boar, who had been walking on the river bottom, now felt it give way under him, so that he was obliged to swim. The weight of so many passengers pushed him lower.

"I'm so glad you joined us, Toby," said Susannah.

"Unfortunately," choked Toby, "when I step out of Mother Weather-sky's garden, I shall disappear. Magician's orders, you know."

He could go no farther. His head bobbed under the water, just as those on his back gave a joyful cry.

Before them glittered the golden tree. Its fiery leaves shimmered; its golden bark dazzled their eyes. Golden bells sparkled and chimed on every branch, and there, in all that blinding brightness, gleamed the golden door.

"Have you got the key?" gasped Toby as he struggled for footing on the roots that glowed under the dark water.

Anatole scrambled off, and trembling with excitement, he fitted the key to the lock. The hinges gave a musical sigh as the door sprang open. Sunlight streamed over the threshold and down a green corridor.

"Give me your hand, please," called Susannah.

She was struggling on the slippery roots, trying to reach the door. Behind them on the riverbank Mother Weather-sky stopped shaking her stick and hurled it straight at Susannah. As Anatole stretched out his hand, he heard the shattering of glass. Mother Weather-sky gave a terrible laugh, and he found himself holding a hand as warm as his own.

He saw before him a little girl who looked exactly like Susannah. But she was not made of glass. She wore a green velvet gown and a green ribbon in her hair, and the whistle around her neck was a real blade of grass looped on a chain of forget-me-nots.

"Where is Susannah?" asked Captain Lark, bewildered.

"Here," said the girl. "Don't you know me?"

"Don't dawdle over miracles," called Plumpet's voice from beyond the threshold, "for I think we have found the King and Queen at last."

Everyone, even Toby, followed the cat down the corridor into a round green room, so magically furnished that Anatole thought that of all the marvels they met on their travels, this was the very best. Moss and wild strawberries tapestried the walls, which gave off a delicious scent of wild thyme and freshly cut grass. From the ceiling hung a small green castle cut from a single emerald, in which a light shone and lit up a company of dancing couples within, each a different-colored jewel given human shape, just as a real castle might appear to shepherds gazing at it from a distant hillside.

But the most remarkable sight was the fragrant bed of rosemary that grew in the middle of the room, on which lay a man and woman elegantly dressed in green robes, their hands folded, their eyes closed. On the man's head grew a crown of fennel, as green as if it had seen nothing but sun all its days.

Susannah rushed to them, knelt down, and kissed them. Then she rubbed their hands. And the others, seeing that she could not wake the sleepers, greeted them with "Time to rise" and "Top o' the morning to you" and other cheerful expressions, but all their efforts failed.

"The whistle," said Anatole. "Blow the whistle."

Susannah put the blade of grass to her lips and blew a loud clear note.

Nothing changed. She blew a second time.

Then the walls of the tree began to grow lighter and thinner. The man and the woman opened their eyes and sat up and looked at each other.

"I had such a peculiar dream," said the man, helping his wife to her feet.

"And so had I," she told him.

"Mother! Father!" cried Susannah. Then she turned to her companions. "*These* are my true parents. The spell is broken!"

Now the tree was gone and they were all standing together on a bridge over the river in the open air. The Queen of the Grass put her arms around Susannah.

"Are these friends of yours, Daisy?" she asked.

"My name isn't Daisy now. My friends gave me a new one," answered the girl gravely. "My name is Susannah."

And she began to tell her father and mother the whole story. But when she mentioned the rabbit, she paused in surprise.

"Why, what has become of Captain Lark?" she asked.

Where the rabbit had been leaning on his wooden leg only a moment before, they saw a man in a sailor suit, examining his two sound legs and rubbing his short brown hair and carefully touching his pale, modest ears.

"I am Captain Lark," he said, "and I'm as hale as the day I set forth on my maiden voyage. Look sharp, children. I've my own face at last."

Behind him a handsome young man in green doublet and hose stepped forward. First he embraced the King, then the Queen, and then Susannah.

"Toby, at your service," he said. Tears of joy shone on his cheeks. "Come into the garden. The spell is broken."

It was marigold time in the garden, and on both sides of the river stretched a sea of gold, dotted by men and women, all in green, who moved slowly toward them, as in a dance. Behind them rose a golden castle.

"Where are the figureheads? Where are the broken ships?" Anatole whispered.

The King pointed to the sky, blue and clear save for one gray cloud in which could be seen, very faintly, the shape of a tiny woman in a green cape, beating the air with her stick. When the cloud broke into pieces, she disappeared.

"Is she gone for good?" asked Anatole.

"From our island, yes," said the King of the Grass.

"And where is her house?" asked Captain Lark.

"She hasn't one," replied the Queen. "She never did have one till the Magician came."

"Papa, who are the people coming this way?" asked Susannah.

"They are the people who live in the garden," said the King. "Let's go and meet them."

Then there was such rejoicing that it seemed to Anatole as if everyone on the island were celebrating a birthday. The castle of the King and Queen was built entirely of sod, planted with flowers, so that every wall and turret was a garden in itself. Marigolds covered the castle from top to bottom. Hedges of silvery green artemisia, taller than Anatole had seen it growing at home, led from the main door into an intricate labyrinth of terraces and fountains. Exploring the grounds at the back of the castle, Anatole came upon a row of marigold kennels and was at first alarmed to see Mother Weather-sky's dogs taking their ease in the yard.

"You'd better not try anything funny," he warned the Great Dane, keeping a safe distance from his old tormentor. "The King and Queen are back, you know."

The Great Dane only wagged his tail.

"So you've changed too," said Anatole. "You've gotten smaller somehow. And more friendly."

In front of the castle, tablecloths had been spread on the grass and laid with platters of apples and grapes, and bowls of butter and cream, and loaves of bread that steamed when you cut them open. The men and women of the court came eagerly forward to pay their respects to the King and Queen and the guests of honor. Captain Lark sat at the Queen's right hand, Plumpet sat at the King's left, so that she could have a good view of him, because as she said later, "A cat may look at a king, and I don't know when I shall ever have another opportunity." Quicksilver padded to and fro, snuffling up a little of everything, to the great amusement of Toby. Anatole and Susannah walked among the courtiers, greeting them; everyone wanted to hug Susannah and to shake Anatole's hand.

When Captain Lark saw the two children coming to join him at last, he bowed and said, "I have decided to stay here forever. The King of the Grass has made me captain of the royal navy."

"We haven't a navy yet," said the King, laughing, "but if we should ever need one, Captain Lark will be in charge of it. Tell me, Anatole, would you like to be my son and live on our island? It is always summer here, and though you will grow up, you will never grow old."

Stay here on the island? Anatole tried to imagine such a life, warm, pleasant, but without his mother to sing him songs, his father to play soccer with him in the front yard, his grandmother to tell him stories of when his mother was a child and of her own childhood, so many years before he was born.

"Thank you very much," said Anatole, "but I would like to go home. What I really want is some of the fennel that grows in your crown. We had a hard winter, and my grandmother's fennel didn't come up this year."

"So my daughter tells me," said the King.

He reached up, lifted a fragrant clump from his crown, and handed it to Anatole.

"Oh," said the boy, "you've made a great hole in your crown!"

"It will grow together again," the King assured him.

Even while he was speaking, a new shoot appeared, unfolded its leaves, and closed the gap.

"Plant it as soon as possible when you get home," said Toby.

"How do I get home?" asked Anatole.

The Queen leaned toward him and pointed to a row of silvery green hedges that wound from where they sat toward the horizon.

"In the Magician's labyrinth, people lost their way. In ours, they will find it again. Take the path that starts from the castle."

"How long should I follow it?"

"Till you reach home," answered the Queen.

"I wish very much you could stay with us," said the King.

"And so do I," said Susannah. "Don't forget me, Anatole." She took from her neck the grass whistle on its chain of forget-me-nots and put it around his neck. "When you whistle on the grass, I shall hear you and know you are thinking of us."

Captain Lark was too much overcome to say a word. He whisked a large handkerchief from his pocket, blew his nose fiercely, and hugged first Anatole and then Plumpet. He even hugged Quicksilver, who wiggled all over with pleasure, for never in his life had anyone shown him so much affection.

"SHE TOOK FROM HER NECK THE GRASS WHISTLE ON ITS CHAIN OF
FORGET-ME-NOTS AND PUT IT AROUND HIS NECK."

Plumpet offered her paw, rather solemnly, to the King and Queen and Susannah, and then to Toby, who presented her with a bouquet of catnip. This moved her so much that she forgot the fine speech she had prepared for the occasion and could only say, "I shall include you in my memoirs. Your names will be household words among cats."

"I shall miss you," said Anatole, "all of you."

Holding Quicksilver, he started down the path the Queen had shown him. Glancing over his shoulder and waving as he walked while Plumpet scampered at his heels, he saw his friends' hands waving back, like the bright crests of waves moving farther and farther away from him, until the hedges grew so high that he lost sight of them altogether. Before he had time to regret it, a tiny bird, feathered in gold, darted out of the hedge and lighted on his shoulder.

"Good-bye, Anatole," it chirped. "Thanks to you, I'm free again."

"Have we met before?" asked Anatole, puzzled, for he did not remember ever having seen such a bird.

The bird laughed.

"How could I meet you when I've never left you? I am the road to Mother Weather-sky's garden, and nobody will ever need me again."

"You don't look much like a road," said Plumpet.

"I almost never look like a road," sang the bird. "Sometimes I look like a lizard, leading you into moonlight.

Sometimes I look like a blossom turning to stone on the water. Good-bye!"

Before Anatole could say thank you, the bird flew off. But the boy could hear it singing, "This way! This way!" and he ran after it, his eyes scanning the sky for a last glimpse of it, so that he hardly knew where his feet carried him—

12.

—until he ran straight into his grandmother's clothes-line.

Grandmother was walking in her garden.

"Look here—the fennel's come back after all," she said, pointing to it. "And I've a nice surprise for you. Your parents sent you a kind of barometer from London. It's called a 'weather house.' Where have you been all morning?"

Anatole did not answer, only followed his grand-mother into the dining room. There on the table stood a little house with two doorways. In one doorway stood an old woman, in the other doorway stood an old man. The man wore a crown of leaves and carried a staff wound with flowers and crowned with a grasshopper. The woman carried a quiver of lightning bolts on her back and leaned on a stick. Both figures were nicely carved and painted green, except for their faces, which were so hastily done you could scarcely make out the expressions.

"It says on the bottom of the house that *she* comes out when it rains and *he* comes out when it's fair," said Grandma. "Tomorrow let's change their places, out of fairness to the old woman."

"It's no use changing their places," said Anatole. "Mother Weather-sky always brings storms."

Beside the weather house stood Quicksilver, one side bright, the other side dark, waiting for somebody to polish him. Plumpet was asleep in the middle of the table.

"We'll have a late lunch today," said Grandmother. "We can't use the table until Plumpet wakes up. But I found a bird's nest in the lilac bush while you were gone. And the snake grass has come up. When I was a girl, we used to whistle on snake grass. I wonder if I can still do it since I lost my teeth?"

The whistle! Anatole looked down. There was nothing around his neck but a smudge of dirt, which did not escape Grandma's notice.

"Did you wash up before you went to bed last night?"

The last thing Anatole wanted to do was wash up.

Through the French doors the sun was shaking lights like coins over the honeysuckle bush while the cardinals whistled to each other in the pear trees.

"Mother Weather-sky is in, and the King of the Grass is out," said Anatole. "Come on, Grandma. It's a perfect day for exploring."

Uncle Terrible

"...HE CROUCHED DOWN AND BROUGHT HIS EAR CLOSE TO UNCLE
TERRIBLE..."

I .

Outside the train window, the early morning mist was rising from the river and rolling over the land so that the hills seemed to be smoking. Anatole held his breath. "Hold your breath when you pass a graveyard," the kids on the school bus always chanted, "or you'll be there soon." But he could not hold it long enough to pass this one.

"Is that Himmel Hill?" asked a nun seated across the aisle, and she pointed out Anatole's window.

"Sure is," said the conductor. "We don't stop there if we can help it."

Then they rushed into total darkness. Anatole's mouth felt dry, and his father's words, as he waved good-bye, came back to him: "If Uncle Terrible isn't there when the train pulls in, call your mother and me right away."

Anatole opened his knapsack, took out his comics, and counted them. Six comics: *Thor, Spiderman, Captain America, The Legion of Superheroes, The Fantastic Four, The Incredible Hulk.* All in mint condition. Uncle Terrible would accept them, read them, and return them to Anatole. And maybe he would give Anatole some of the comics he bought for himself.

The train stopped so abruptly that everyone lurched forward. There was a general scramble for suitcases. Anatole clutched his knapsack and followed the nun into the aisle, where a throng of passengers was moving slowly toward the door.

"You have quite a collection of comics," she observed, smiling down at him.

"They're not mine," said Anatole. "They're a present for Uncle Terrible."

The nun stared at him. "How old is your uncle?"

"He's not my uncle. He's a family friend. And he's— grown up," added Anatole, realizing that he did not know Uncle Terrible's age.

"What did you say your friend's name was?" she asked.

"Uncle Terrible. Because"—and now it was Anatole's turn to smile—"because he's so terribly nice."

Anatole watched her step down to the platform and disappear into the crowd of strangers, and suddenly he felt he had lost his last friend. He touched his back pocket to check on his glasses. "Four eyes, four eyes," the kids at school called him. He had quit wearing them after that, but he always carried them.

"Is someone meeting you?" asked the conductor as he helped Anatole down the steps.

"Yes. No—I—"

Among the bustle of passengers getting off, somebody was hurrying down the platform toward the train and combing his thick black hair with his fingers: a large man, in faded jeans, a tweed jacket, a shirt as red as a fire truck, and rainbow suspenders, into which he had tucked his black beard like an ascot.

"Uncle Terrible!"

The man lurched forward, seized Anatole under the arms, and lifted him into a hug. His beard was as soft as a cat and smelled of cigars.

"Thank goodness you've come," said Uncle Terrible. "The apartment is like a tomb. An Egyptian tomb, crammed with treasures. This morning I actually lost myself between the kitchen and the bedroom. Anatole, where would you look for your Self if you lost it?"

He took Anatole's hand as they walked so that they would not be parted by the men and women rushing past them.

"I've invented a new game, Anatole. This is your Self—" and Uncle Terrible held up a gold button with a lion embossed on it. "Now, close your eyes. In which of my one hundred pockets have I hidden you?"

"Let's find a quieter place to play, Uncle Terrible," suggested Anatole.

"We'll play at lunch," said Uncle Terrible.

Outside the station, warm rain was beginning to fall. Everyone except Anatole and Uncle Terrible scurried for shelter. The two friends strolled past the shops, ducking from awning to awning. A few windows still showed masks and paper pumpkins, though Halloween had come and gone two weeks before.

They passed a window, empty of all but the sign:

MAMA'S HEROS, HOTDOGS, SUBMARINES

"Closed," said Uncle Terrible. "What a shame!"

In the window of the bar next door, Tarzan burst into light over the pinball machine. Bells clanged, balls clattered and spun, bim! bim! Through the half-open door drifted a strong smell of beer.

"For lunch," said Uncle Terrible, "I fancy a chocolate cat."

Anatole half expected Uncle Terrible to pull a chocolate cat from one of his pockets. But instead, his friend paused in front of a revolving door and pushed Anatole gently ahead of him.

After the bustle of the street, the boy was glad to sit at one of the small tables, close to a showcase of corn muffins and chocolate cats. The coffee shop was full of people. They sipped their coffee or waited in line at the counter, for this was a bakery as well as a coffee shop. Two girls behind the counter drew string from a golden ball that hung from the ceiling, with which they tied parcel after parcel, quick as shoelaces.

"Your order, sir," a plump girl said to Uncle Terrible.

Uncle Terrible ordered two chocolate cats and a bowl of whipped cream. As the girl started to leave, he called after her, "And bring me one of those apples from the bowl on the counter, please."

Then he turned to Anatole. "I mustn't neglect your health, or your mother won't let you visit me again. Now, where did I put that gold button?"

He took off his jacket. The lining drooped with pockets, and pockets lined the front of his vest, so that he seemed to be full of doors, like an apartment building.

"What a wonderful vest!" said Anatole, quite forgetting about the gold button.

"Do you like it?" asked Uncle Terrible, quite forgetting about it also. "It was knitted for me by a tailor on twelve golden needles. His grandfather got them from the emperor of China. Ah, the apple has arrived."

"Aren't you having an apple, Uncle Terrible?"

"I shall have a little nibble of yours."

He took a very small bite, as if he were eating poison.

Anatole shivered. It's my wet sneakers, he thought, and he could almost hear his mother saying, "Anatole, didn't I tell you to wear your boots?" At that moment he felt a tap on his shoulder.

"...HE...REMINDED ANATOLE OF A HERON THAT...COCKS ITS HEAD
AND SCANS THE WATER FOR FISH."

A man with red hair and a red beard and a long neck was bending toward him, holding out a paper fan of the sort that does not conveniently fold into one's pocket, and the way he hunched into his shabby fur coat reminded Anatole of a heron that crooks its neck and cocks its head and scans the water for fish.

One side of the fan was painted with dragons, the other with this brief message:

I AM A FAN OF ARCIMBOLDO THE MARVELOUS,
179 WEST BROADWAY.
YOUR WISH IS MY COMMAND.
MAGIC SHOWS EVERY NIGHT, 7 AND 9.

"You do not feel the need of a fan now," said the stranger, "but later, on a hot day, when all creation can scarcely draw a breath, you will remember your fan, and you will fan yourself, slowly at first, then faster and faster, and you will thank Arcimboldo from the bottom of your heart. I am Arcimboldo the Marvelous."

At the next table, an old woman was setting a shopping bag on the table. Her fur coat was all tight gray curls—just as if it had gotten a permanent, thought Anatole. She plunked herself into a chair, kicked off her boots, and massaged her bare feet.

"I came in all the way from Brooklyn to pick up my new dress, and it's still not ready," she said to Uncle Terrible, just as if they were old friends. "Cicero Yin is a good tailor, but is he worth it?" She turned to Arcimboldo. "Sometimes I wish I had wings instead of feet."

Arcimboldo the Marvelous muttered to himself. It sounded to Anatole like "I want my dinner" or "I'm growing thinner." To Anatole's astonishment, the woman vanished before his eyes, like a flame that Arcimboldo had blown out. A little brown and white barn owl hopped from her empty chair to the table and cried in a mournful voice, "Whoooooooo! Whoooooooo!"

All around them, people shielded their faces with their arms, and the girls wrapping parcels behind the counter sank to their knees in terror.

"Open the door!"

The door was flung open, and the owl circled the room twice and flew out into the world.

When Anatole glanced around for Arcimboldo the Marvelous, the old man, too, was gone.

2.

he city is full of magic," said Uncle Terrible, "but rest assured, Anatole, that women do not turn into birds. Perhaps it flew in from the kitchen." He paused on the dark landing and puffed a little. "That was stair number eighty-eight. We have eleven more to go."

Anatole leaned over the banister. It wound down, down, like a far-off road, all the way back to the first floor. A milky light sifted through the skylight overhead, where someone had hung a dozen spider plants that trailed their branches toward them.

At the top of the last landing were two doors.

"Mine's the left one," said Uncle Terrible.

He took a large key from one of his pockets and fitted it into the lock.

"Why do you have two keyholes, one so high up?"

"You mean the peephole? That shows me who's on the other side of the door before I open it," replied Uncle Terrible. "Open sesame!"

And with a turn of the key, the door sprang open.

"Behold," said Uncle Terrible.

In the middle of the room, rising out of a sea of newspapers, old grocery bags, and dirty laundry, stood a doll's house. It was taller than Anatole; it was nearly as tall as Uncle Terrible himself. Built of rosy brick, it had a widow's walk on the roof and a front door, dark blue, with a round brass knocker that glimmered like a friendly moon, and French doors tall enough to walk through—if you were small enough.

"Oh, Uncle Terrible!"

"A gift from an unknown admirer," said Uncle Terrible. "I found it on the fire escape. I asked around the building if anyone had lost a house, but no one claimed it. Welcome to my quiet retreat from—" and he waved his arms at the disorder of the apartment, as if he were commanding it to disappear.

"Let me show you around," he said, and he took a very small key from a very small pocket in his vest and unlocked the front door of the little house. The door did not open. But the entire front of the house swung open, like the door of a cupboard.

Anatole could scarcely believe his eyes. Three master bedrooms, each with a canopy bed, and a living room with a ruby glass chandelier and a sofa upholstered in red silk, and a large kitchen painted in red, white, and blue, and a bathroom—why, the bathtub was *gold!* It crouched on four feet that ended in silver claws.

The most remarkable room was the library, just off the kitchen. At the table in the center, a dozen mice could have dined in comfort and afterward stretched out on the purple plush carpet for a nap, or curled up in one of the two armchairs, upholstered in leather. To Anatole's delight, the bookshelves were crammed with books, yet the largest volume was no bigger than a postage stamp. The boy took down a green one and opened it. The cover was soft and brilliant as moss, and the lines of the text lay close together, like strands of hair.

"Uncle Terrible, have you a magnifying glass?"

"I have no magnifying glass strong enough for that book. Put it back."

He sounded so disturbed that Anatole felt he should never have asked. For the first time that day, he wanted to go home. Uncle Terrible broke the silence between them.

"If you want to wash up for dinner—" He touched a faucet in the bathroom, and a pearly thread of water flowed into the silver sink. "Hot and cold," he announced proudly. "The stove in the kitchen works too. You can cook a small dinner for one large person, or a large dinner for six small persons. And in the evening—" He pressed a button in the living room, and the whole house lit up from top to bottom. The ruby chandelier glittered, throwing tiny rainbows on the ceiling like confetti.

"I used to have two chandeliers," Uncle Terrible observed. "The other was made of emerald glass. One night the emerald chandelier simply vanished. Make yourself at home, Anatole. I have to straighten up the outside world."

And he bustled about the big room, stuffing clothes into drawers, pushing boxes into closets, and as if by magic there came into view a four-foot inflatable King Kong by the front door and a Frankenstein mask on the wall and a comfortable jumble of overstuffed chairs and a floor lamp with an awful tasseled shade and an African violet on a pedestal and a red plush sofa that reminded Anatole of a kindly old man with a sagging belly.

Just in front of the little house, something gleamed through a knot in the floorboards. Anatole put his eye to it. To his disappointment, another eye did not meet his.

"Uncle Terrible, you have a blue marble under your floor. Let's rescue it."

Uncle Terrible shook his head. "We'd have to pry up the boards, and that would disturb the cockroaches. I sweep all my cookie crumbs into that crack, and the cockroaches never bother me. We've had the arrangement for years."

"May I call them cockroaches too, Uncle Terrible?"

"Why, what else would you call them?"

"Mom calls them Martian mosquitoes. If you say, 'I just saw a Martian mosquito in the kitchen,' nobody will know you have cockroaches."

"But why shouldn't people know? Everybody in the city has cockroaches. The people who think they don't have them have the polite kind that mind their own business. Let me show you your bedroom. It connects to the bathroom. You won't mind my tiptoeing past you during the night? Give me your knapsack."

Beside the brass bed in the back room was a roll-top desk. Wham! Uncle Terrible, who was a high school Latin teacher, pulled the top down on a Latin dictionary and a clutter of papers, and now the room was perfectly tidy.

"A lovely view of the fire escape," said Uncle Terrible, pointing to the window. "And if you want a night light, you can borrow my Statue of Liberty."

There she stood, on top of the desk, gazing out the window.

"Can I pick her up?"

"Of course. Can you read the fine print on the base?"

Anatole read it easily: "Give me your tired, your poor, your huddled masses yearning to breathe free."

"You know, the first penny I ever earned came from my Polish grandmother," said Uncle Terrible, "and she gave it to me for learning the rest of that poem by heart."

"Poem?" said Anatole, puzzled.

Uncle Terrible gravely recited it:

"Not like the brazen giant of Greek fame,
With conquering limbs astride from land to land;
Here at our sea-washed, sunset gates shall stand
A mighty woman with a torch, whose flame
Is the imprisoned lightning, and her name
Mother of Exiles. From her beacon-hand
Glows world-wide welcome; her mild eyes com-
      mand
The air-bridged harbor that twin cities frame.
'Keep, ancient lands, your storied pomp!' cries she
With silent lips. 'Give me your tired, your poor,
Your huddled masses yearning to breathe free,
The wretched refuse of your teeming shore.
Send these, the homeless, tempest-tost to me.
I lift my lamp beside the golden door!'"

"Very nice," said Anatole, though he was not sure he understood it.

"Now I want you to listen carefully, Anatole," said Uncle Terrible. "We're clean out of milk, and I'm going to the store at the end of the block. I won't be gone more than twenty minutes. Don't open the door to anyone but me."

"I promise," agreed Anatole. "Can I play with the little house?"

"Yes. But don't turn anything on. And don't touch the books. Here. Have a stick of bubble gum."

"My mom said—"

"It's sugarless," said Uncle Terrible.

"Thanks," said Anatole, and he popped the gum in his mouth.

As he knelt by the little house, he could hear Uncle Terrible humming his favorite tune, "Blue Moon." His footsteps grew fainter and fainter. Anatole opened the door of the oven and discovered a pile of dirty dishes. The plates were the size of buttons, the coffee pot no taller than a thimble. To Anatole's surprise, the oven was warm.

But he had promised he wouldn't turn on the oven, or the stove, or the lights, or the water.

But he could explore the apartment. Where would Uncle Terrible sleep? On the sofa, probably. He had given Anatole his own bed.

Anatole opened the door nearest the sofa. Uncle Terrible's jackets hung in a row, like a parade of ghosts. The smell of cigars still clung to them. How funny to have so many jackets! Anatole had only his windbreaker with the souvenir patches. None of Uncle Terrible's jackets had souvenir patches.

He opened a high thin door in the kitchen, and a little ironing board dropped out as far as its hinge would allow and struck him on the shoulder.

He opened the door beside the awful tasseled lamp, and a bed sprang out. It too was fixed at one end of the wall. So this was where Uncle Terrible slept. Anatole pushed the bed up, and to his relief it folded itself away obligingly, and he shut the door on it.

He opened a fourth door beside the pot-bellied sofa. Ah, this was where Uncle Terrible kept his comics! Four columns of comics that reached all the way to Anatole's waist. He sat down on the floor and plucked one from the top of the neatest column. *What if Doctor Strange had served Dormammu instead of the Ancient One?*

Mint condition. He turned to the first story.

Thump, thump.

What if Uncle Terrible came back and found him messing up his comics?

Thump.

But that wasn't a footstep on the stairs. The noise came from the opposite direction.

Thump.

From his room.

Thump, thump.

He shoved the comics into the closet, jumped up, and was just closing the door when a high voice outside the window sang,

> "My father is a butcher,
> My mother cuts the meat,
> And I'm a little wienie
> That runs around the street.
> How many times
> Did I run around the street?
> One, two, three—"

Anatole ran into his bedroom, unlocked the window, pushed it open, and crawled out on the fire escape. Drops of rain hung glistening from the railing. A tiger cat stared at him with sad eyes as if to warn him, "*Go back, go back, home is best,*" before it scampered away.

At the top of the fire escape, a girl in her nightgown was skipping rope. When she caught sight of Anatole, she called down, "I heard you talking. Are you sick, too?"

"No," Anatole called back.

"Why aren't you in school?"

"We're on holiday. What's wrong with you?"

"I have the flu!" shouted the girl. "And I'm so bored. When Grandma comes back from the store, I'll have to go back to bed."

Skip, skip.

"My name is Rosemarie, and my grandma has a garden on the roof. Come on up. I'm mostly well."

Anatole paused, halfway up the stairs.

"Uncle Terrible told me not to let any strangers in the house."

"Grandma told me the same thing," said the girl. "We'll play outside."

She darted back up to the roof, her black braids blowing behind her.

The fire escape shook so violently that Anatole did not dare look down, for he could see through the steps into the alley nine flights below.

"The roof," said the girl, "is the best place of all."

There were tubs of geraniums and pots of chives. Both grew as thick as in his mother's garden at home, and just such a pebbly path led through her garden as snaked among the pots and tubs in this one.

But his mother did not have a stone table and two wooden benches and half a great blue tub turned on its end with the Virgin Mary inside holding out her hands, and his mother didn't have a grape arbor, thickly woven with stems and bunches of grapes, both green and purple, hanging inside. Anatole reached for a grape, but the girl grabbed his arm.

"They're not real," she said. "But our doves are real. Come and see our doves."

The doves lived in a snug little tower like a pagoda. It had hundreds of windows through which the doves could come and go, though none were to be seen just then. But Anatole could hear them, cooing inside, and when the girl opened the door, there sat the doves on their nests, some white, some brown, and each family in its own room. The birds blinked at the children and clucked and scolded, and the girl closed the door again.

"I saw an owl in a coffee shop today," said Anatole. "And I met a magician. He gave me a fan with dragons on it."

He was tempted to add that he had seen a woman turn into that owl before his very eyes, but Uncle Terrible had said women never turned into birds. She *had* disappeared though. Very likely into the ladies' room.

"An owl? Was it tame?"

"No, it flew outside."

"Maybe we'll see it," said the girl.

From the garden they could look out over other roof-

"ANATOLE REACHED FOR A GRAPE, BUT THE GIRL GRABBED HIS ARM."

tops into a forest of television antennas and ventilation shafts. They could look right into other people's windows. They could look down at the cars, small enough to fit in their hands. Then they could look beyond the buildings to the river and the train tracks and the turrets of Himmel Hill.

Close by, bells began to chime. The girl pointed across the street to a church and a schoolyard next door. Children were running in from recess.

"That's my school," said the girl. "I hate it. We aren't allowed to talk during lunch, and we have to say catechism every morning with Sister Helen."

Suddenly Anatole caught sight of a familiar figure in a tweed jacket and a red shirt and rainbow suspenders crossing the street toward them.

"I have to go home," he said, "right now."

As he ran down the steps, the girl called after him, "I've always wanted a fan with dragons on it."

"I'll leave it for you on the fire escape," Anatole called over his shoulder.

After a frantic search, he spied the fan behind the little house. He stuck it to the fire escape with his bubble gum and was fumbling with the lock on the window when he heard someone fumbling with the lock on the door and Uncle Terrible strode into the apartment, his arms full of groceries. Anatole hurried to meet him.

"I've been thinking," exclaimed Uncle Terrible, "that it's a great afternoon to visit the Guinness Book of World

Records Museum. And we can take dinner at a little place I know that serves the best spaghetti in town."

After dinner Anatole was tired but also content, for it isn't every day you can try on the belt of the fattest man and afterward eat all the spaghetti you want for supper. Though at home he never went to bed before nine, he did not object when at seven o'clock Uncle Terrible announced bedtime for both of them and unfolded his own bed in the living room. He graciously accepted Anatole's gift of comics and promised to let Anatole pick six from his own collection, in fair trade. He had left a book on mummies by Anatole's bed and a silver bell and a glass of milk and a box of Fig Newtons, and he told the boy he could turn on the Statue of Liberty and sleep in his clothes, including his baseball cap, and he could read as late as he liked.

But he must stay in his room. On no account should he open his door after eight o'clock.

In an emergency he might ring the bell.

Yes, that was fine with Anatole. He pulled on his jacket and climbed into bed, examined all the photographs of mummies in the book, thought how much he would like to have one, and turned off the overhead light. He thought how delightful Latin would be if he had Uncle Terrible for a teacher. The Statue of Liberty glowed, as if a star had fallen into the room.

If he were home, his father would sing to him before he turned off the light.

"Get on board, little children," Anatole sang to himself, since there was no one to sing it for him.

He dozed off at last.

He had scarcely fallen asleep when a clap of thunder woke him—bang! bang! The rain roared down, the window blew open, the door flew open, and Anatole jumped out of bed to close it.

What was that faint light in the living room? Was Uncle Terrible awake? Was he ill? No, not ill.

He crept into the living room. The light came from the little house.

3.

In the little house, Uncle Terrible sat at the kitchen table humming "Blue Moon" and holding the moss-green book in his hand. He was shading it with a bouquet.

"Why, that's the book he told me nobody could read," said Anatole. And he rushed forward. "Uncle Terrible, make me small too!"

The tiny gentleman sprang from his chair.

"Make me small, too, Uncle Terrible. Make me small, too!"

Uncle Terrible's legs seemed to fold under him. He sank into his chair, clutching his head. Presently he turned to Anatole and spoke, but alas!—his voice was as small as his person. Anatole could scarcely hear him, though he crouched down and brought his ear close to Uncle Terrible, who raised himself on tiptoes and rested one hand on Anatole's ear lobe to steady himself.

"If you promise me that you will never, never tell anyone, I shall reveal my secret," said the faint, whiskery voice of Uncle Terrible.

"I promise," said Anatole.

"Please don't shout."

"I'm not shouting," said Anatole. "This is my normal voice."

"It is not normal to me," squeaked Uncle Terrible. "Now listen closely—and stay away from that crack in the floor. On the first page of this book you will find some lines written in an unknown tongue. Read them out loud."

"But you said I couldn't—"

"I said you couldn't read them with a magnifying glass. You can read them by the light of these flowers."

Anatole took the flowers from Uncle Terrible. Cornflowers and clover, they gave off a faint fragrance that reminded him of a place he had known long ago but could not quite recall. He opened the book, held the flowers over the first page, and found that he could read the text perfectly.

"Woneka, wonodo,
Eka mathaka rata,"

said Anatole.

There rose to his nostrils a delicious promise of toast.

"A gbae se—"

He noticed that Uncle Terrible was covering his ears, and he lowered his voice.

"Dombra, dombra, dombra."

Fall, small, and away! Anatole gazed around in astonishment at the cupboard, the table, the stove, and the grill, on which half a dozen sandwiches were sizzling. Uncle Terrible was tucking the bouquet into the pages of the book.

"Would you like a toasted cheese?" he asked. "I'm simply famished."

If the little house seemed wonderful before, it was ten times more wonderful now when Anatole turned and looked back at the apartment. The awful tasseled lamp shaded the little house like an ancient tree; the hooked rug unfolded range upon range of hills and valleys like waves lapping away into the darkness.

"Uncle Terrible," said Anatole, "are you a magician?"

"No," said Uncle Terrible. "I'm just lucky."

He arranged the sandwiches on a plate and carried

them to the kitchen table and drew up stools for Anatole and himself.

"The day after my other chandelier disappeared, some unknown benefactor left this book on my shelf. When I opened it, the bouquet of pressed flowers fell out, and when I picked up the flowers, they came alive in my hand, and I discovered the book was magic."

Uncle Terrible took a large bite of his sandwich.

"What other spells can the book do?" asked Anatole, who was much too excited to eat.

"That's what I'd like to know," said Uncle Terrible, chewing. "Every night I read it to myself—I don't dare read it aloud anymore—but I can't crack the code. It's not Latin, it's not Greek, it's not Finnish or Sanskrit. Come— let me show you something you'll like."

And he ushered Anatole into the library. A checkerboard was set up on the center table.

"I love checkers," said Anatole.

They drew up chairs, and Anatole had just made the opening move when they both heard a rustling in the kitchen. Uncle Terrible stood up, and Anatole stood up, and they tiptoed to the door.

Nobody there. But the thud of something being lugged over the floor could be heard in the living room. Anatole felt as if his heart were pounding in his throat. Nevertheless, he followed Uncle Terrible into the living room.

A cockroach in a turban of wrapped tinsel, a tinsel skirt, and a gray cloak was trying to fasten a broken candle to the hook that had once held the missing chandelier. She had made a loop in the wick to hang it by, but one claw held something under her cloak as she worked, and this greatly hampered her. The other she snapped and clicked: the sound sent shivers up Anatole's spine.

"Bring back my chandelier!" shouted Uncle Terrible.

With a volley of loud squeaks, the cockroach leaped out of the house and fled into the darkness of the apartment. Anatole was certain he had never seen any creature as monstrous as this one.

"What a mess!" said Uncle Terrible. "Crumbs all over. I suppose she helped herself in the kitchen."

The grilled cheese sandwiches were gone.

"I'd feel safer if I were my own size again," said Anatole.

"I understand perfectly," said Uncle Terrible. "Now, where did I put the magic book?"

Suddenly he glanced down and gave a shriek. "There it is—down the crack in the floor!"

Anatole knelt beside Uncle Terrible at the edge of the crack, which yawned vast as a canyon to them now.

"I don't see it," said Anatole.

"It was there a minute ago," said Uncle Terrible.

A thin slice of light gleamed up at them from under the floorboards.

"Let's tie the bed sheets into a rope," said Uncle Terrible, "and I shall lower you into the crack."

"Me!" exclaimed Anatole.

"My dear boy, there's nothing to fear. At the first tug, I shall draw you up."

"BEYOND THE BLUE MARBLE LAY A LOW COUNTER, AND BEHIND
THE COUNTER DOZED THE COCKROACH..."

It did not take them long to pull the sheets off the beds and knot them together. Anatole grasped one end, and Uncle Terrible held the other and lowered him down, down through the crack, till the boy's feet rested on a pile of dust, not far from the blue marble.

Oh, how big the little space in the crack looked to him now! Beyond the blue marble lay a low counter, and behind the counter dozed the cockroach, still wearing her turban of wrapped tinsel and her gray fur coat, which had once belonged to a mouse. Sandwich crumbs clung to her feelers, which drooped across her front legs; she had fallen asleep reading a moss-green book that Anatole recognized only too well. He found himself more curious than frightened.

A silver ring in the shape of a snake sparkled on a shelf directly over her head.

"That ring is much too large for a cockroach," said Anatole, forgetting that in his present shape it was also much too large for him.

He reached over the sleeping cockroach and took down the ring. Neatly inked on a stamp hinge attached to the ring were the words:

FINDERS KEEPERS

"I've found it, so I'll keep it," said Anatole. He slipped the serpent ring over his arm. "If Uncle Terrible says I ought not to keep it, I can always send it down the crack."

Over the cockroach's head glowed an emerald

chandelier, the very match of that hanging in the living room of the little house, and its light showed Anatole shelf upon shelf—he couldn't see the end of them, for they seemed to stretch into infinity—and they were crammed with paper clips, postage stamps, holy medals, razor blades tied in packets of a dozen or so, two plastic grapes that Anatole recognized as having come from the roof garden, and assorted marbles, mostly cat's-eyes and aggies, smaller than the blue marble, though just as beautiful.

From the top shelf hung a sign:

THE TRADING POST
OPEN ALL NIGHT

And below it, embroidered in purple thread on a scrap of lavender silk:

THOU SHALT NOT STEAL

Anatole picked up a smoky-glass marble. Tiny gold stars glittered deep at the heart, like lights at the bottom of a well. The price tag read:

2 CENTS

"I'll send two pennies down the crack tomorrow," said Anatole, and he took the marble.

Then he laid hands on the book.

"It can't be stealing, since the book belongs to Uncle Terrible."

Holding his breath, he slid the book very slowly out from under the head and bristly legs of the sleeping cockroach. Then he hurried back to the blue marble and grabbed the bed sheet.

"Uncle Terrible, Uncle Terrible—pull me up!"

Greatly excited, Uncle Terrible jerked the rope so hard that Anatole dropped the glass marble, which clattered against the blue one, and both rolled past the counter toward the far end of the shop.

The cockroach lifted her head in time to see the boy's feet disappear over the edge of the crack. "Thief! Thief!" she cried.

A general scratching and scuttling answered her in the upper world of the apartment. From the darkness under beds and the darkness under bureaus, from the darkness under the icebox and the darkness under the stove marched the cockroaches, hundreds upon hundreds, and each cockroach carried an open safety pin, and the pins glittered, and the popping eyes of the cockroaches glittered, and they surged into the living room like a wave wearing diamonds on its back.

"Uncle Terrible, hurry! Say the spell!"

Uncle Terrible seized the book and clutched the bouquet over it.

"Woneka, wonodo,
Eka mathaka rata,

A gbae se
Dombra, dombra, dombra."

As Uncle Terrible soared to his full height, he tossed both book and bouquet to Anatole, who caught them and read,

"Woneka, wonodo."

At which one cockroach, larger than the rest, shouted, "Brothers and sisters, attack!"

Fifty cockroaches leaped on the boy and tried to grab the book. Anatole hung on, and while the cockroaches pulled and tugged, he managed to keep both book and bouquet out of their reach and to shout,

"Eka mathaka rata,
A gbae se
Dombra, dombra, dombra,"

just as the page tore and the biggest cockroach fled through the crack with the book between his teeth and the flowers between his feelers, and all the cockroaches poured after him like sand sifting down a hole.

And now, silence. Still trembling, Anatole switched on the tasseled lamp in the living room of the apartment. Uncle Terrible was sitting on the sofa, his eyes closed, his palm on his forehead.

"I lost the book, Uncle Terrible," said Anatole, "but I saved this ring."

He handed the ring to Uncle Terrible. What a cunning silver serpent it was, bright and modest as starlight.

Uncle Terrible tipped it this way and that, till the light caught an inscription on the inside:

IF LOST, TURN TO THE WRIGHT
WRIGHTS SUPERIOR TOFFEES LTD.

"A souvenir of Anatole's battle with the Martian mosquitoes," said Uncle Terrible as he slipped the ring over his own right pinky. "There, now we won't lose it. What we need, Anatole, is some hot chocolate to revive us after our ordeal."

The ring glimmered and shimmered and wreathed his finger so exactly like a real snake that Anatole couldn't resist stroking it, for he was fond of snakes and often kept garter snakes as pets. He stroked it once. Twice.

On the third stroke, an extraordinary change came over Uncle Terrible. His body pulled itself out like taffy and gathered itself to the thickness of Anatole's wrist. The rainbow suspenders and the red shirt dissolved to an iridescent shimmer on the gorgeous skin of a snake that lifted its head and met Anatole's astonished gaze. The ring clattered to the floor. Uncle Terrible no longer had hands to hold it.

4.

he snake made a sound like steam hissing
and darted its tongue in an experimental sort of way.

"Oh, Uncle Terrible," cried Anatole, "I'm sorry!"

"Sssssorry, ssssorrrry," breathed the snake and draped
itself around the boy's shoulder. It had Uncle Terrible's
face, right down to his black beard, only the face was small
as an apple and peered out from a hood of glittering scales.

"Sssssave the sssssilver sssssserpent," hissed Uncle
Terrible.

"I don't know how to save you," wailed Anatole.

"The sssssilver ssssserpent," repeated Uncle Terrible.

"The ring?"

Anatole picked it up and read the inscription aloud once more. "'If lost, turn to the Wright.' I'm not lost, Uncle Terrible, but you are. So I'll turn to—to the right."

He turned and found himself facing the mirror.

"Maybe I should turn the ring to the right?"

And he slipped the ring over his finger.

"Sssssstop," warned Uncle Terrible, but Anatole was already twisting it.

The light in the little house gathered itself into a beam that shone straight into the mirror, like a road. And there in the mirror itself—what was that prick of light advancing slowly, like a train at the far end of a tunnel? He squinted, shaded his eyes, and gave a gasp of delight.

A stagecoach, no higher than his knee, was jogging toward him. It was made of moss and drawn by a ghostly mule. Smoke wrapped around a ladder of bones; you could see right through him.

"Why, there's no driver," exclaimed Anatole, for he saw none.

But who else could be singing so loud and joyously?

"Great eye, little eye, great eye can see,
Little eye is sharp eye, little I will be.
Little eye, simple eye, little eye is free,
Little eye is sharp eye, little I will be."

Swaying to and fro on the driver's seat, a star-nosed mole was beating time with the reins, though he was scarcely as big as the boy's hand, which is bigger than most moles but smaller than most drivers. On the side of the coach facing Anatole, forget-me-nots grew in the shape of a sign:

MOTHER'S TAXI

BY APPOINTMENT TO DAME KIND

NO SPELL TOO LARGE   NO FOLK TOO SMALL

"All aboard," called the mole. "Plenty of room inside."

He dropped the reins, and the mule halted above the pedestal, just over Uncle Terrible's African violet. The coach rested so easily on the air that it might have stood on a well-traveled road. The mule stretched forth his neck to browse among the blossoms and pawed the air as if he felt under him the lush grass of an invisible pasture.

"I didn't call a taxi," said Anatole.

The mole peered at Anatole over his pince-nez, from which a black ribbon dangled, thin as a whisker.

"Didn't an enchantment take place?" asked the mole.

"It sure did," said Anatole. "Uncle Terrible accidentally turned himself into a snake. But I didn't call a taxi."

"Whenever an enchantment takes place," said the mole, "it rings up the main office, and I'm sent out. I'm the porter, taxi driver, stretcher-bearer, and comforter, all in one. Are you enchanted, lad?"

Anatole shook his head.

"Then you can ride up on the driver's box with me."

The mole scampered down and opened the door of the coach; the moist fragrance of a summer night breathed out of it.

"Sssssssssir," began Uncle Terrible, but the mole interrupted him.

"Can't talk, eh? Once we get moving, you'll find your voice. In you go, my scaly friend."

Uncle Terrible flashed inside, and the door closed so seamlessly after him that you could not have told where to open it again. Anatole climbed up beside the mole, and found to his surprise that he was exactly the right size for the coach. The mole jerked the reins, and the mule lifted his head and trotted around the room at a brisk pace, still chewing. Yet the violets, Anatole noticed, were untouched.

"Aren't you going back through the mirror?" asked Anatole.

"Never go out the way you came in. It's in the rules."

"Whose rules?" asked Anatole.

"Mother's rules."

"Your mother made that rule?"

"She's not just my mother," said the mole.

"Whose mother is she?"

"When you meet her," said the mole, "you can see whose mother she is. Draw the curtain from the window behind you, lad."

Anatole did so and could not help smiling. In the coach Uncle Terrible lay curled up on an upholstery of fresh roses. On the opposite seat perched a brown and white owl.

"That passenger met Arcimboldo in a coffee shop on Tenth Street," said the mole. "She'd stopped at the tailor's to pick up a dress, and she was on her way back to Brooklyn. She told me that nobody's heard of Arcimboldo the Marvelous in Brooklyn, so of course she wasn't on her guard when they met."

Anatole remembered the woman with the tired feet in the coffee shop and said to himself, "So she really did turn into an owl."

"Now, the passenger sitting next to her had fair warning," continued the mole.

"There's nobody next to the owl," said Anatole.

"You are mistaken. The other passenger is invisible except for that little rope she carries. The poor girl was given a fan"—and here Anatole nearly fell off the box— "and it has Arcimboldo's name right on it, but do you think she took the slightest notice of that? No, indeed. She started fanning herself, and both she and the fan faded into thin air. He's not called Arcimboldo the Marvelous for nothing."

"Rosemarie!" exclaimed Anatole.

The coach sailed through the open window, over the fire escape.

There, on the bottom step of the fire escape—that's where I left the fan for Rosemarie, thought Anatole.

The coach climbed steadily into the wind, and Anatole drew his jacket around him. Below him the roof garden lay dark and still, but the rest of the city, a patchwork of rectangles, was stitched with light.

"And how did your companion fall into an enchantment?" inquired the mole.

"Uncle Terrible? This ring did it," answered Anatole, and he held out his hand.

The mole glanced at the ring and said, "It's the same story everywhere. Arcimboldo loves to put spells on ordinary things. The toys in Crackerjack, the keys in people's pockets, the catsup in diners. He loves to make trouble. He loves to put innocent people under his spells. Once they're in his power, nobody ever sees them again."

The mole sighed, then turned shyly to Anatole. "Tell me, lad, do you know any stories? I dearly love stories."

"What kind of stories?" asked Anatole.

"True stories," said the mole.

"Let me tell you what happened to me and Uncle Terrible tonight," said Anatole, and he told the mole all about the little house and the magic book, and how a cockroach in a turban snatched it, and how Anatole went after the book and lost it.

"I like the part about the book best," said the mole. "It's so mysterious, the way it appears in the library after Uncle Terrible loses his emerald chandelier."

"I suppose the cockroaches traded the one for the other," said Anatole. "The book must be one of Arcimboldo's tricks."

"Moss green, with flowers to light the pages? That's not Arcimboldo's book. This land was full of magic long before you and I came to live on it, and once in a blue moon something magic turns up. I suspect one of Mother's winds brought your companion his little house. Long ago on Himmel Hill, wonderful toys marked the graves of children, and living children played there, so the dead wouldn't be forgotten..." His voice dwindled away. He cleared his throat. "Don't miss the view."

They passed over the twin towers of the World Trade Center, as humble as salt and pepper shakers. Then the coach turned sharply and headed north.

"Where's the George Washington Bridge?" asked Anatole.

"Just where it always was," answered the mole. "But in Mother's taxi, we see by different lights. I follow the stars. Bridges come and bridges go, but the stars have been showing the way to Mother's house for thousands of years. You have a bird's-eye view, lad, and the birds see a great deal more than those who live on the ground."

Anatole peered down into the darkness. The land was all forest and pasture, and it seethed and rustled with life. Hundreds of creatures flowed across it; mice and ferrets, chipmunks and snakes. In the clearings, tortoises, coyotes, badgers, and woodchucks ran together. Deer leaped in herds, cougars loped side by side, and mountain goats ran peacefully alongside them.

Level with the coach, a flock of geese were winging north.

"Old honkers, aren't you flying the wrong way?" called the mole.

"Mother called us, Mother called us," answered the geese.

"Where are they going?" asked Anatole.

The coach sank slowly toward a hill crowned with white stones, some straight like steeples, some round and thin as slices of bread, and all standing silent like pieces in a game abandoned by giants.

"I hope we're not going to the graveyard," whispered Anatole.

The mole sang on over the squeaking and mewing and roaring and rumbling of the animals:

> "The least of Mother's errands
> is good enough for me.
> It's more than I am worthy of—"

as the coach floated over the iron gates and the mule's hooves brushed the tops of the gravestones.

> "I want nothing better.
> I'll not exchange it
> For anything greater."

Now they were skimming row upon row of American flags that marked the graves of the veterans of many wars. How skillfully the mole guided the mule between granite angels and moss-shrouded soldiers in heroic poses, and how gently the mule alighted before a plain marker of modest size, on which was inscribed in raised letters:

"...AS THE COACH FLOATED OVER THE IRON GATES AND THE MULE'S
HOOVES BRUSHED THE TOPS OF THE GRAVESTONES."

MOTHER

The mule lifted his hoof and knocked three times on the stone. The animals crowded around him, the door of the coach swung open, and the scaly form of Uncle Terrible writhed out, followed by the owl.

"My dear Anatole," he whispered, "I've had a most interesting conversation with a young lady who claims that you made her invisible."

"I can speak for myself," said Rosemarie's voice close by.

"Hush," rumbled an elk. "Mother's coming."

The earth around the gravestones grew lighter and lighter, as if a fire burned in the heart of each of them.

"Windows!" exclaimed Anatole. "The ground is full of windows."

The windows, which kept the odd shapes of the stones themselves, looked right down into Mother's house. The shape of an angel gave Anatole a clear view of the living room. In the fireplace, so tall and deep that Anatole could have walked right into it, a lively flame was leaping and sending its smoke up through the ground.

And now the boy observed that the smoke of many fireplaces in many rooms was rising all over the grave-yard, and he remembered noticing this smoke from the train window and mistaking it for mist.

The lamp on the great round table was carved from a rutabaga, and the oil in the lamp threw such an amber light on the floor that the rushes scattered there seemed washed in honey.

"Do I spy a newspaper on the table?" asked Uncle Terrible. "Do I see *The Christian Science Monitor*? Who on earth brings you *The Christian Science Monitor*?"

"Nobody," said the mule. "It blew here years and years ago. Out of date, of course, but what does that matter? The creatures come. They can't read a newspaper, but they expect one, they want one. Especially the mice. They've worked in the lobbies of the best hotels, and they have their own notions of grandeur. Mother doesn't want to disappoint them."

"The bedrooms are even better than the living room," a bear murmured into Anatole's ear. "Mother has the best beds in the world, especially if you're planning to hibernate. She made them herself from the wood of the Himmel tree, and they tell the most lovely stories."

"Where do the Himmel trees grow?" asked Rosemarie's voice.

The bear gazed respectfully at the empty space that was Rosemarie.

"There are no more Himmel trees. The early settlers cut them down for cradles."

"And what language do the beds speak?" asked Uncle Terrible.

"Your language," replied the bear.

And Uncle Terrible, who did not hear well, said, "Ur language! I fear the stories would be lost on me."

Suddenly voices from within the house sang,

"Sweep the floor, sweep the floor,
Mother's hurrying toward the door."

A restlessness rippled through the creatures. The light from the stone bearing her name brightened into a door.

"Here comes Mother!" squeaked a raccoon.

All turned. A giant of a woman was striding toward them. The face that smiled out of her sunbonnet was as lumpy and plain as a potato. She wore corn shucks gathered into a gown, over which shimmered an apron of onion skins. Through her bonnet poked antlers that branched out like a tree, and at the end of every branch danced a flame, which lit the ground before her. She was carrying a wicker basket from which every now and then she threw a handful of white roses. The roses melted as soon as they touched the ground, and a thin glaze of frost sparkled in their place.

"Is my table set?" shouted Mother.

"Yes, Mother!" chorused hundreds of voices from within.

"Is my soup ready?"

"Yes, Mother!" called the voices as before.

"Then I'm ready," she answered, and through the door she crawled on all fours, with the animals and Anatole and Uncle Terrible and Rosemarie and the owl tumbling in after her.

5.

Around the stone table gathered the creatures, and when Mother took her place, a flurry of chipmunks actually scampered across the table and crowded into the folds of her gown.

"Would you prefer a seat among the snakes?" the mole asked politely.

"Certainly not," said Uncle Terrible.

An elk marched round and round, keeping order, especially among the rabbits, who were inclined to be rowdy. Anatole and Uncle Terrible and Rosemarie, whose skip rope was visible in her invisible hand, sat between the mole and the raccoon, both of whom kept a sharp eye on her place so that nobody would sit on her.

"Children, children, are you hungry?" said Mother.

A hubbub of squeaks and roars answered her, and the otters thumped their tails on the table. Mother walked around the table, and as she walked, she raised her right hand and out dropped suet for the cardinals, sunflower seeds for the chickadees, and thistle seeds for the finches. She raised it again, and a dozen bundles of hay dropped in front of the deer. She raised it again, and a mess of fish fell in front of the otters—oh, nobody was forgotten, nobody, nobody—and Mother bustled back and forth, encouraging the coyotes to take seconds and the eagle to clean his plate and the quails and the pheasants to try a new dish she had invented just for them.

When she came to Anatole, she stopped walking and clapped her hands for silence. "My dear children," said Mother, "we have among us three guests whom Arcimboldo the Marvelous has enchanted. I need not tell them what I must tell you, that we are all in grave danger."

A deep hush fell over the company.

"Since the beginning of time, I have worn at my waist two threads twisted into one, the thread of life and the thread of death. Every morning you have heard me sing the 'Song of Strong Knots' to keep them in place."

"Thank you, Mother," said the elk.

"Alas for us! One of my children gave Arcimboldo that song. And Arcimboldo learned it so well that he could sing it forward and backward. And when he sang it backward, the threads of life and death untwined themselves and flew into his hands."

"It was the cockroaches," the mole whispered to Anatole. "They generally sit near me, and they're absent."

"Now Arcimboldo has taken the thread of life to be knitted into a cloak," continued Mother. "When he puts on that cloak, I will be helpless to break his spells."

"Is there no one who can help us?" bellowed the old otter with gray whiskers.

Silence. Then a tiny voice piped up, "We spiders know, if we haven't forgotten."

A brown spider crawled to the middle of the table, and all the creatures leaned forward to listen.

"Our old lore says, Let a great hero win the thread of death, let the thread be knitted into a cloak, and let the cloak of death be joined to the cloak of life, and all whom Arcimboldo has enchanted will be whole again."

"Can you spiders do this?" asked Mother.

"Our old lore says, Whoever wants it must win it," squeaked the spider. "And the hero must be human."

Everybody looked at Anatole.

"You're human," said the otter. "You can't deny it."

"I'm no hero," said Anatole. "I'm scared stiff."

"Nobody is a hero before the quest," said Mother.

"And where will he find the cloak of life?" asked the mole.

"It is being knitted on the twelve golden needles of an innocent tailor who has no idea what a wonderful thread he's got under his roof," said Mother.

"Golden needles? It's not the tailor who lives on Tenth Street?" exclaimed Uncle Terrible.

"The very fellow," replied Mother.

"And maybe the only honest man in the city," said the spider. "Nobody who steals or lies can command the twelve golden needles."

"I know the fellow," said Uncle Terrible. "Anatole, take me with you."

"And take me, too," said Rosemarie. "I'm a great knitter. I can do cable stitch. And take the owl, she's very clever—why, where is the owl?"

But the owl who had chatted so amiably in the coach was nowhere to be found.

"Our old lore says that the great hero must go alone," said the spider.

"Oh, bother your old lore," hissed Uncle Terrible.

"Look here," said Anatole. "I don't even know where the magician lives."

Mother pointed to the fire.

"My fireplace is so deep that you can easily walk behind the flames. Anatole, tell me what you see behind the fire."

"A door," replied Anatole.

"Through that door," said Mother, "you will find a road. It will take you to my elder trees. And on my elder trees I hang my masks. From sunrise till dawn of the following

"SHE FOLDED HER BIG HAND AROUND HIS SMALL ONE AND LED HIM
BEHIND THE FLAMES..."

day, you can be a jackal, a mouse, a wolf, a dove, a cat—
whatever pleases you. Take only one. You will know the
right time to wear it."

She folded her big hand around his small one and led
him behind the flames, and he thought he had never
been so hot in all his life. And there crouched the tiger
cat he had seen on the fire escape outside Uncle Terrible's
apartment.

"I didn't know *you'd* be here," said Anatole.

"Home is best," purred the cat.

When Mother pushed the door open, the smell of
moss and clover cooled him a little.

"The road runs through my orchard and leads straight
to the magician's house. My mule will take you to the
border. You'll find him grazing in the orchard."

Anatole turned to say good-bye, but Mother stopped him.

"Don't look back," she warned him.

The last sound he heard as he stepped through the
door was the tiger cat wailing in a singsong voice,

> "Anatole will come, will come,
> Witchcraft will be set a-going;
> Wizards will be at full speed,
> Running in every pass.
> Avoid the road, children, children!"

The door hushed closed behind him. East, west, north
—as far as he could see—grew apple trees. Their branches
were laden with fruit, and under one of them, browsing

in the tall grass for windfall apples, waited the ghost-mule.

"Walk or ride?" he inquired.

"I can walk, thank you," said Anatole, for the mule looked very tired.

"If I were in your shoes"—here the mule glanced down at Anatole's sneakers with their broken and knotted laces—"I'd ride. We've a long journey ahead of us. But suit yourself."

"If it's very long, I think I will ride," said Anatole, and the mule stooped and Anatole clambered on. The mule's back felt sharp as a saddle of sticks, and the boy thought he had never sat so uncomfortably in all his life.

"Take a little refreshment," said the mule, "where my heart used to be."

Anatole peered down into the mule's rib cage, and there, where his heart used to be, hung a little basket. He drew up the basket and found a sandwich, neatly wrapped in grape leaves, and a mug of hot soup.

"Mother put 'em there," said the mule. "I hope you like peanut butter?"

"Oh, very much," said Anatole.

"And the soup was made fresh today. She gives it only to travelers. It warms, it strengthens, and it doesn't spill."

Orioles and goldfinches glittered in the trees, meadowlarks and catbirds sang in the thickets, the tall grass trembled, and the daisies and cornflowers nodded as the travelers passed.

"I'm no end of convenience to Mother," the mule said, in pleased tones.

Anatole wiped his mouth on the back of his hand and was seized with remorse. "I'm so sorry—I forgot to offer you any," he said.

"No matter," said the mule. "I don't eat things, I just whiff off the fragrance, though when I had my flesh, I had appetite enough. My old master sold fish, and I pulled the wagon through good times and bad times. But it was always my wish to find Mother. And the last day of my life—awfully cold, it was—I opened my eyes and there was this giant of a woman lifting the gate to my stall. 'What do you want?' I says to her. 'A ride home,' she says to me. 'I can't carry you,' I says. 'Didn't say you had to,' she says, and she picks me up and tucks me under her arm and walks right out into the yard. I felt as light as a leaf, and she never put me down till we got home. And I've been a great convenience to her ever since."

Now the apple trees grew scarcer; they were entering a grove of elders. A wind shook the branches, and Anatole saw that what he had taken for leaves were masks: coyotes, badgers, tigers, elephants, toucans, pelicans, with empty spaces left for the eyes.

"Let's see what's left," mused the mule.

"Don't people steal them?" asked Anatole.

"Nobody comes here without Mother's leave," said the mule, "and once the masks are used, they always come home to Mother. What pleases you?"

The mule strolled under the trees so that Anatole could choose.

"I like the tiger," said Anatole.

"If I were in your skin," said the mule, "I'd pick the cat. Fierce but friendly. Small but quick. At home everywhere."

Anatole saw the wisdom of this and pulled off the mask of a black-and-white cat, which instantly shriveled itself into a thin loop around his wrist.

"When you need it, it'll be waiting for you. Mother's masks take care of themselves."

He trotted out of the grove into a sparse woods. And it seemed to Anatole that the trees were less friendly on this side, the air chillier. The sky shone red, as if the sun were setting.

"Red sky in the morning, sailors take warning," said Anatole.

"The sky is always red over Arcimboldo's house," observed the mule.

They were once again passing through an orchard. But no birds sang here, and no fragrance of flowers, or of apples crushed underfoot, delighted them. In the trees, made of steel with copper leaves, hung dozens of ruby balls. There was a smell of pennies hoarded in jars, the silence of jewels under glass.

"No matter how he tries," said the mule, "Arcimboldo can't make an orchard like Mother's. I can't go farther than this. His house is just beyond these trees."

Terror seized Anatole when he saw the mule was leaving him. "What will I say to Arcimboldo? What can I say? And how will I find the thread of death?"

"Our old lore says—" whispered a voice.

And the brown spider sprang to the top of the mule's head.

"Little brother!" exclaimed the mule, very much surprised. "Does Mother know you're here?"

"What does your old lore say?" asked Anatole.

"Our old lore says that the magician will ask you to play a game of checkers. Do you play checkers?"

"A little," faltered Anatole.

"Then you must outwit him. Arcimboldo's glasses let him peer around the corners of time. He can see your next move before you make it, and your next move, and your next. If you can get him to take off his glasses, you have a fair chance of winning. And if you win, ask for the thread of death."

"And what happens if I lose?"

"Don't ask," said the spider.

"But I want to know," said Anatole.

The spider brushed a sparkle of web off one leg.

"This I learned from Mother's well.
Fifteen years a mourning bell,"

buzzed the spider. "A bell in Arcimboldo's house. That's what you'll be."

A clatter of wings in a tree behind them made them turn in time to see the owl darting through the still branches.

"As the owl flies," said the spider, "you'll find the magician's house."

"The blessings of the sun and moon and rain and stars and snow and spiders and my old bones be upon you," said the mule. "And that's more than Arcimboldo has. Good-bye."

6.

When he stepped into the clearing, Anatole found himself facing the oddest house he had ever seen. The outer wall was copper, engraved with hundreds of doors, and each door glowed as if burnished with secret fires. And what did the wall enclose? An enormous steel dome, without windows or chimneys or any sign of life.

As he walked around the wall, he couldn't help admiring the doors engraved on it, some plain, some overgrown with fruit and flowers drawn in the most

meticulous detail. On one especially ornate door was in-
cised a bellpull and a door knocker in the shape of a
wreath.

"So many doors, and not one of them opens," Anatole
said with a sigh.

No sooner had he spoken than the head of Arcimboldo grinned at him through the leaves of the wreath.
"Ring the bell, Anatole, ring the bell," cackled the head.

Anatole felt a pair of claws grip his right shoulder.
He spun round, terrified. Perched on his shoulder was
the owl.

The boy now saw a real bell hanging on a copper ribbon. Before he could reach for it, the bell started to ring
by itself, and as if waiting for that signal, bells began to
ring around him, though he could see nary a one of
them: families of church bells, choruses of dinner bells,
sleigh bells, school bells, cowbells, ship bells, and bells
that boomed out the hours in a hundred town clocks, all
of them telling a different time, all of them invisible.
And it seemed to Anatole that under the jangling he
heard weeping. Over the ringing of the bells and the
weeping roared the voice of Arcimboldo.

"Ring the bell, Anatole, ring the bell!"

This time Anatole gave the bell at the door a good
hard tug. Instantly the ringing stopped. The head of Arcimboldo vanished. The engraved door opened, and
Anatole felt himself pushed inside.

The room was very hot, and smooth and windowless
as an egg. By the light of the seven giant rubies that hung

from seven copper chains, the walls gleamed a fiery rose. There was not much furniture. In the middle of the room glimmered a little silver table and two benches, one encrusted with emeralds, the other with pearls. The checkerboard was also cut from emeralds and pearls, as well as the playing pieces. Against the far wall stood a copper chest, and next to that a fireplace, but no fire burned there.

"The bells, Anatole," said the owl on his shoulder.

Around the room, in midair, hung the bells—hundreds and hundreds. And in them he saw not his own reflection but the shapes of creatures that seemed to be hidden in the bells themselves. Bloodhounds and tomcats, rabbits and hedgehogs, a girl carrying a trombone, a man taking off his overcoat, a baby asleep in its stroller, robins and deer—rows and rows of them, silent in the fiery light.

Anatole sat down on the bench covered with pearls and longed for the strength of Superman, the web-slinging fingers of Spiderman, and the nimble feet of the Human Fly. How easy to be a superhero when you had special powers! And how impossible when you were only human.

Presently he heard a crash. He jumped up in time to see a leg dressed in silver shoes and striped stockings tumble down the chimney and hop beside the chair, where it stood at attention.

Bing-bang-bong! A second leg dropped down and, flexing itself, bounded over to the first.

Hsshhhh! The copper chest sprang open, and out popped a left arm and a right arm, both sleeved in green velvet. They fluttered to the chair with a swimming motion and drifted a short distance above the legs.

Thump. Out of the chest toppled the torso, in a doublet of green feathers. It settled itself on the legs and allowed the arms to join it, one at each side.

"I hope you play checkers," said Arcimboldo's voice, close by.

"Yes," quavered Anatole, "but couldn't you please put on your head?"

"You know, I was sure you'd run away," continued the voice. "And if you run, you forfeit the game."

From the ceiling floated the head of a green bird with a long, sharp beak.

"When I'm at home, I wear my real head," explained Arcimboldo.

He took a pair of gold-rimmed glasses from his doublet and set them carefully on his beak. From the glasses dangled a silver string. He unfastened the string very carefully and tossed it to the owl, who caught it in her beak and flew from Anatole's shoulder to Arcimboldo's.

"If you want the thread of death, you must win it fair and square," said the magician.

"Did you win it fair and square?" asked Anatole.

"I bought the secret of winning it from a cockroach," answered Arcimboldo. "I gave him all the gold he could carry."

And he tapped the golden cockroach that swung on a

"FROM THE CEILING FLOATED THE HEAD OF A GREEN BIRD
WITH A LONG, SHARP BEAK."

thin chain around his neck. A cockroach in a turban and a ragged coat; Anatole recognized her at once as the mistress of the Trading Post.

"Never trust a traitor," said Arcimboldo, "not even a helpful traitor. The first move is yours, Anatole."

Anatole put out his hand to make the first move and hesitated.

"Just a minute, Arcimboldo. If you get to wear your magic glasses, I get to wear my magic glasses. That's fair and square."

"Your magic glasses?" exclaimed Arcimboldo, frowning.

"I wouldn't be caught dead without my magic glasses," said Anatole. And he took his glasses out of his pocket and put them on.

Then, with a great show of confidence, he moved his first piece one square.

"Arcimboldo, I'm sorry for you. I'm not called 'Four Eyes the Fierce' for nothing."

Arcimboldo studied the board and stole glances at his opponent's face. The boy was smiling.

"Anatole, I'm sorry for you, too. So sorry, in fact, that I'm willing to play without my magic glasses if you'll play without yours."

"Not a chance," said Anatole.

"Fair and square, Anatole. We play without glasses or we don't play."

"Oh, Arcimboldo," said Anatole, "you don't know what you're asking."

"No glasses, or no game."

"We must take them off together, then. One, two, three."

At the count of three, both took off their glasses and tucked them out of sight. Anatole squinted at the board, though in truth he saw it very well, for he was near-sighted and could always see what was close to him. The army of pearl checkers shone on the emerald squares. Arcimboldo's emerald pieces glowed sullenly, green on green.

"Emeralds for me. Pearls for you," said Arcimboldo.

The silence in the room deepened. It seemed to Anatole that everything in the room, from the largest church bell to the smallest sleigh bell, was holding its breath.

Arcimboldo moved an emerald. "Your turn," he said.

Anatole was about to make his move when a crackling and a sizzling all around him made him draw back in alarm. Before his eyes, Arcimboldo turned into one giant flame, which danced on the emerald bench and gave off the most terrible heat. A faint moaning and humming swept through the bells. The owl beat her wings, and the searing wind they stirred took Anatole's breath away.

"Do you feel the need of a fan now, Anatole, when all creation can scarcely draw a breath?" whispered the magician. "Oh, if you had that fan now, you would thank Arcimboldo from the bottom of your heart."

Anatole was too parched to speak. It took all his strength to move a single pearl. The instant he did so, a roar as of rushing water filled the room. The fire sizzled out without leaving so much as a single ash, and now

there whirled about on Arcimboldo's bench a giant waterspout, which sent wave after wave into the room. The
bells rocked and clanged in muffled voices, and the table,
the chest, the benches, and the checkerboard were tossed
up and down. The waves broke over Anatole's head,
pulled him into their churning depths, and threw him
out again, but he clung to his seat and shouted, "Your
turn, Arcimboldo—your turn!"

The waves retreated, the waterspout vanished, and
Anatole saw, as Arcimboldo took on his own shape and
made his move, that not a single piece on the board had
been disturbed. Anatole took one of the magician's emeralds, the magician took one of Anatole's pearls. In a
silence so total that every sound in the universe seemed
to have withdrawn from this place, Anatole and Arcimboldo played the game out till only a few pieces remained
on the board.

"Your turn, Anatole."

When Anatole lifted his hand to move, a blast of cold
air froze him to his seat. He tried to think of his next
move, but his head felt crammed with pictures, as if
somebody inside were turning the pages of a vast book.
Here was Uncle Terrible's apartment and the little house,
and here was the Trading Post under the floorboards and
the rutabaga lamp in Mother's house, and here was his
own mother kissing him good-bye and his father kissing
him also and saying, "Take my knapsack, Anatole, take
my knapsack!"

"Your move, Anatole," said Arcimboldo. "What a

splendid bell you'll make! I shall hang you in a place of honor."

Ice glittered on the walls and on the wings of the owl and on the bells—and what was Arcimboldo himself now but an iceberg, turning slowly on the bench, sending out its cold breath to freeze him?

Place of honor, place of honor. The words repeated themselves in Anatole's head. He looked down hopefully at the board. His own breath sent little clouds of steam over it.

Thump, thump. Was Rosemarie here, skipping invisibly among the bells?

No. It was the racing of his own heart.

Thump.

The emeralds on the board flashed at him. He thought of Uncle Terrible, imprisoned in the body of the serpent, and how cold the world would be without him. And without Rosemarie. His mind cleared, and he made his last move. The pearl took the last emerald on the board. Over the pealing of bells he heard himself shouting, "I've won, Arcimboldo. I've won!"

"Fair and square," sneered Arcimboldo. And he gave a long mocking laugh. Anatole saw a door open, and the owl, clasping the thread of death in her beak, fluttered into the air and sailed outside.

Anatole jumped up and ran after her. When he crossed the threshold, he was blinded by the brilliance of trees. Steel they were—bark, branches, all steel—and on every tree hung ivory apples that gleamed through the copper leaves like young moons ripening under the red sky. The owl was skimming the tops of the trees.

All at once she wheeled back, as if something had caught her eye, and alighted in a steel thicket ahead of him. He heard a shriek, a hiss, a beating of wings, and much crashing about in the underbush.

The owl uttered a mournful whistle and flew off toward the magician's house, but Anatole could see that she no longer carried the thread in her beak. Then Anatole heard a voice call after her, "That will teach you to eat your betters, madam."

To Anatole's astonishment, the voice began humming "Blue Moon." Parting the branches, he spied a snake on whose skin shimmered all the colors of the rainbow, sunning himself by a small pool.

"Uncle Terrible!" shouted Anatole.

Startled into a panic, the snake fled straight into the pool.

"Come back," called Anatole, and he plunged his hands into the water after it. To his dismay, the silver serpent ring slid from his finger and sank as swiftly as if summoned by the water itself.

The next moment, out crawled Uncle Terrible.

"Oh, marvelous pool!" cried Uncle Terrible. "Whoopee!"

Nothing was left of the snake but its skin, draped over Uncle Terrible's arm.

"Uncle Terrible, I'm so glad you're here."

"And so am I, Anatole. You didn't see me, following you in the orchard?"

Anatole shook his head.

"The thread of death," said Uncle Terrible. "Do you have the thread of death?"

"The owl must have dropped it," said Anatole.

Uncle Terrible threw away the snakeskin, and they began to search on hands and knees. Presently a kindly voice inquired, "Is it silver?"

Anatole and Uncle Terrible looked at each other in alarm.

"Is it silver?" repeated the voice. "Of course, I've no use for silver. You've nothing to fear from me."

Suddenly they both saw the thread, half covered by the snakeskin, sparkling on a fern.

"Arcimboldo is playing a trick on us," whispered Anatole.

"He doesn't need to play any more tricks," said Uncle Terrible. "He knows we'll never find our way out."

The voice spoke again.

"I believe I could fly you out. You still don't see me? I'm right at your feet."

At their feet rested the fern.

"Do the plants in this forest talk?" exclaimed Anatole.

"I don't know," said the fern, very humbly. "These are the first words I've ever said to anyone."

"Perhaps the snakeskin—" began Uncle Terrible.

And Anatole, who was also thinking of the snakeskin, lifted it away and said to the fern, "Speak."

The fern was mute. Anatole laid the snakeskin on it once more.

"Can you speak now?"

"As I was saying," continued the fern, "I come from a large family. Do you see my relatives waving all around the pool? Gather some of us together and bind us into wings with your silver thread."

"What if the wings don't work?" mused Uncle Terrible.

"Oh, but Uncle Terrible," said Anatole, "what if they *do*?"

7.

On the headstone next to Mother's house, a skip rope was turning in the moonlight, and the thump, thump of invisible feet echoed in the rooms below. The animals did not mind, any more than they minded when the squirrels clucked in their sleep or the cock crowed at false dawn, waking everyone up, and then again at real dawn, waking everyone up all over again. The last sound they listened for was the voice of the invisible girl singing them into oblivion:

"Bottom, bottom, dish clout,
Dutch cheese and sauerkraut.
Our first lieutenant was so neat
He stopped in the battle to wash his feet."

The possums, who had never seen a lieutenant, spread the rumor that the first lieutenant—and the ancestor of all other lieutenants—had had a pink snout and a long thin tail like theirs. The tiger cat knew that only a cat would stop in the battle to wash his feet, but he kept this information to himself.

"Igamu, ogamy, box of gold,
A louse on my head was seven years old.
I inched him and pinched him and made his
     back smart,
And if I ever catch him, I'll tear out his heart,"

sang Rosemarie, skipping.

She shared a room with a mole, an elk, and a raccoon. The mole and the raccoon and Rosemarie claimed the bed close to the fire. It was carved to resemble a brake of ferns. The elk, who was a light sleeper, dozed on a fragrant heap of straw, a safe distance from flying sparks.

The mole slept with his glasses perched on his nose and his paws folded together on his stomach. He was always the first to retire. Lying on his back with his eyes shut, he prayed, "Mother of Moles, Father of Ferrets, Sis-

ter of Shrews, Brother of Beavers, Spirit in all of us, whoever you are, bless Anatole. Also, I beg you to improve
my eyesight. Amen."

After the mole had settled himself, Rosemarie hung
her skip rope on the bedpost and curled up beside him
and wished she could grow clothes as soft as his fur.
Then it was the elk's turn. The other two could hear him
pacing round and round, treading the straw flat.

When the raccoon came in, she blew out the lamp.

Last of all, the bed itself would breathe a lullaby that
soothed them like the wind rustling in the leaves that the
bed once had when long ago it grew as a tree on Himmel
Hill.

> "Moonlight, starlight,
> The bogeyman's not out tonight.
> Wash your bones
> With precious stones—"

Soon only Rosemarie lay awake. She listened to the
crackling of the fire and the pleasant bustle of animals in
the surrounding rooms. Through the open door, she
watched the shadows of the nighthawks as they spread
their wings before the Great Fire in Mother's room, not
understanding that the Great Fire warmed everyone in
the house. Rosemarie thought of Anatole and the doves
on the roof at home. She thought of Arcimboldo the
Marvelous, and then she thought of her grandmother,
who did not like to sleep and who made omelets at

midnight and wrote long letters to friends, both dead and alive, and asked Rosemarie to mail them.

At last Rosemarie climbed out of bed, tiptoed past her sleeping friends, picked up her skip rope, and crept up the stairs into the chilly air of the upper world. The raccoon always sensed when she was gone and followed her. He sat on a marble lamb and said, "Don't pay any attention to me. I don't want to make a nuisance of myself."

"You're never a nuisance," said Rosemarie.

Thump, thump, thump. The rope slapped the headstone on which Rosemarie was skipping.

"I'd give anything to know as much as you do, Rosemarie," said the raccoon, sighing.

"You would? Do those rings on your tail come off?"

"In my great-great-grandfather's time, all raccoons could take off their rings. But there's not a raccoon alive today who remembers the way of doing it."

"Now I'm jumping backward with my arms crossed," said Rosemarie.

"You're wonderful. Simply wonderful," said the raccoon.

"Thank you," said Rosemarie.

"It breaks my heart that the otters don't believe in you," said the raccoon. "Except Elder Otter. He believes. The others say you're nothing but an enchanted rope."

"They've got some nerve," said Rosemarie.

"I told them about the wind. I said, 'You don't see the wind, but you see what it does. Our invisible girl is as real as the wind.'"

"I'm a lot realer than the wind," said Rosemarie. "Tell them I've got a mother and a father and a grandmother, and I live in an apartment with a garden, and I go to Sacred Heart Elementary School."

"They'll never believe me. Except Elder Otter."

"Tell them I'm in the advanced math class."

"I'll try," said the raccoon. "If only they'd talk to you at night the way I do."

Thump, thump.

"Will you still talk to me when you can see me?" asked Rosemarie.

"Always and always," replied the raccoon.

"What do you think I look like?"

"You have bright eyes, lovely pointed ears, short silver fur, and a tail more beautiful than I can imagine."

"A tail!" exclaimed Rosemarie.

"Are you laughing at me?" asked the raccoon in sorrowful tones.

"No," said Rosemarie. She was glad the raccoon couldn't see her smiling.

It was Elder Otter who complained to Mother about Rosemarie. He crept to Mother's bed right after the cock crowed at false dawn.

"We all have our little tasks, Mother," he whispered. "We otters fish for you, the rabbits gather greens for your table, the cock puts your lamp to sleep at sunrise, the spiders mend, the elks fetch and carry—oh, I could go on and on. And what does *she* do? She sits by the well and watches the water."

"That's her job," said Mother. "To watch the water."

"Why does she get to watch the water?"

"Because she knows what to watch for."

"You think I don't know what to watch for?"

"Look into the water, Elder Otter, and tell me what you see," said Mother.

Elder Otter scampered to the far corner of Mother's room and crouched at the rim of the well. In that plain room, which held nothing else but the Great Fire dancing in its ring of stones, the well sparkled like an enormous eye.

"What do you see?" asked Mother.

"I see a young trout, more silver than is common, and a pair of young carp, more gold than I'm used to."

"Fish," said Mother. "Is that all you see?"

"That's all there is to see, Mother," said Elder Otter.

"Rosemarie sees more," said Mother. "Rosemarie sees Anatole."

After breakfast, Rosemarie went as usual to Mother's room and sat by the well. She thought of Anatole and of the serpent who called himself Uncle Terrible, and up from the darkness at the bottom of the well swam a picture, which spread itself on the surface of the water like oil. The mole sat beside her to keep her company. Today

"HE CREPT TO MOTHER'S BED RIGHT AFTER THE COCK CROWED AT FALSE
DAWN."

the raccoon joined them, and it was he who first spied two shadows tossing among the stars.

"Mother, Mother!" called the raccoon. "I see Anatole flying! And I see a stranger flying beside him."

"That's Uncle Terrible," said Mother, bending over the water. "He's got his own shape back. He found himself in one of my wells."

"You have wells in the magician's house, Mother?" asked the raccoon, much surprised.

"I have wells everywhere for those who can find them."

Now all four watchers leaned over the image. It quivered a little. In the water-picture, snow was beginning to fall, clearing the street of colors.

"I know that street," said Rosemarie, "but I don't know the name of it."

She was certain she'd passed that blackboard hanging in the shop window, on which was written:

TODAY'S SPECIAL: FLOUNDER!

And the Ebony Beauty Parlor next door, with the face of a black girl framed in a halo of hair. And the tailor shop next door to that:

CICERO YIN, ALTERATIONS

In his window stood a photograph of John F. Kennedy, and behind the photograph a large jade tree spread its plump leaves in all directions.

Under Rosemarie's eager gaze, the two travelers alighted on the roof, several flights above the tailor's shop. She saw Anatole and Uncle Terrible open the skylight and climb in. An owl glided down, peered into the skylight, gave a cluck of satisfaction, and, with a fierce beating of wings, clattered into the air and flew off toward the magician's house.

"She's clumsy," said the raccoon. "She hasn't been an owl long."

"Did she ride in the taxi with me?" asked Rosemarie.

"Yes," said Mother. "And she's going to tell Arcimboldo what she's just seen—what we've just seen."

"She's working for him, then?" asked the raccoon.

The water grew dark once more.

"Can't we help them, Mother?" asked the mole.

"Yes. But we must watch for our chance. Watch. Watch."

8.

natole sat up and rubbed his knee. The room into which they had fallen was very cold and so tiny that when Uncle Terrible stood up, his head brushed the ceiling.

"Are you injured?" asked Uncle Terrible.

"No," said Anatole, and in the same instant both of them saw what had hurt him: a large iron ring anchored to a door in the floor.

Uncle Terrible gave a whoop of joy. Together they grabbed the ring and pulled.

Below them lay another room, much larger, also empty, and another trap door exactly like the first. First Anatole and then Uncle Terrible jumped down and tried to pull open this door also. It did not budge.

"Pull harder," said Uncle Terrible, and the door broke free.

Anatole knelt, and Uncle Terrible squatted beside him, holding it lest it should slam shut and wake the tailor below. A rush of warm air rose to meet them.

They were looking directly into the shop itself. Here was the jade plant and the back of the framed picture of John F. Kennedy, and behind the cash register a partition which hid the workshop from the view of customers. But nothing was hidden from Anatole and Uncle Terrible, who saw below them the tailor's worktable and the pegboard on which he hung his threads, as bright and various as the feathers of birds, and his portable sewing machine and his straight-backed chair. His shears and electric iron gleamed on the worktable. The shelf behind the table was crammed with bolts of cloth and books, which bulged with swatches and patterns. Tacked over the empty clothes rack was a sign:

FINISHED WORK

"Let's go down," said Anatole.

"My dear Anatole," exclaimed Uncle Terrible. "Do you think I'm Superman? Able to leap tall buildings at a single bound?"

"Then I'll go alone," said Anatole. And holding fast to the snakeskin, he climbed through the trap door and let himself down.

He landed—thud!

The spools, the shears, the threads—everything trembled. Out of sight in a room beyond this one, Anatole heard pots and dishes rattle.

"Can you find where he keeps his golden needles?" Uncle Terrible called softly.

Anatole lifted the books and patterns and swatches one after another. Nothing under them but a Chinese newspaper. He peered behind bolts of tweed and twill and gabardine.

Nothing. Nothing.

He tiptoed to the room at the back and found himself in the tailor's kitchen, which smelled pleasantly of ginger. Past the stove, the icebox, the table big enough for one, to yet another door—ah, here was the tailor himself, fast asleep in his bed, his teeth shining in a glass of water on the nightstand.

The tailor sighed and turned over on his stomach. His breathing moved the covers up and down, up and down.

Anatole hurried back to Uncle Terrible.

"I can't find the needles."

"If only the shears could speak," said Uncle Terrible, "or the sewing machine. They'd tell us."

"But they can speak," said Anatole, and he laid the snakeskin on the sewing machine.

The sewing machine gave a hoarse wheeze of astonishment.

"Can you please tell me," said Anatole, "where the tailor keeps his golden knitting needles?"

"Mrrrrsssssrs," answered the machine. "Krrrwww-wooow."

Hastily Anatole took away the snakeskin for fear the machine would wake the tailor and laid it on the peg-board over the threads. The threads all began to chatter at once in shrill voices.

"Can you tell me where the tailor—" began Anatole, but they did not hear him; they had too many quarrels to settle with one another. Again he took the snakeskin away.

"I'll try the shears," he said, feeling rather desperate, for the window showed him the blue light of early morning.

And he laid the snakeskin on the shears.

The shears clip-clapped, once, twice.

"At last," murmured the shears in an oily voice. "At last I'm appreciated. After thirty years of service, I can tell my story."

"Please, can you tell me—"

"I've walked for miles and miles," continued the shears, "up velvet and down linen, over the gabardine highway, along the satin turnpike, and where has it gotten me?" And the shears clapped its two halves together like legs.

"Please," said Anatole. "I need the tailor's golden needles. It's a matter of life and death."

"Can't help you, can't help you," said the shears. "The tailor sleeps with them every night in his pocket, and now he's got them working on a magnificent cape, and he keeps both the needles and cape in bed with him. Keeps an eye on things, keeps an eye on things."

Anatole cast a longing glance at the tailor's bedroom, and the shears clip-clapped once, twice, and said, "If you're thinking of stealing them, think again. They won't go. They'll screech at you, jab you, stab you—oh, think again. They're spoiled things. Brought up among royalty. Think themselves finer than the rest of us."

Anatole considered this remark.

"Does the tailor need an apprentice?" he asked.

"There's only one thing the tailor needs," replied the shears.

"What?" called down Uncle Terrible.

The shears gave a little shriek of alarm.

"Who's that hiding in the ceiling?"

"That's my friend," said Anatole. "You can tell him."

For several minutes the shears would not speak but only clipped the air nervously. At last the oily voice resumed. "A cat. That's what he needs. The mice in this building are driving him crazy."

Anatole felt his right wrist tingle.

"A cat!" repeated Uncle Terrible. "We have no cat. We are undone."

"No, we're not, Uncle Terrible," said Anatole. He held

up his right hand and shook it. Something unwound itself and hung there, grinning.

It was the face of a cat, black from the ears to the nose, with a white chin and two dark spaces for the eyes.

"Mother said if I put it on, I'll be a cat for twenty-four hours," said Anatole.

"Anatole, don't," said Uncle Terrible. "Don't put on that mask."

"Take care of this," said Anatole, and he tossed the snakeskin into the air. It floated up, up, and curled itself into Uncle Terrible's hand. The thread of death he untied from his waist and wound around his finger.

"Anatole—" said Uncle Terrible.

But Anatole was already slipping the mask over his face.

The instant he did so, his ears shrank to pointed tents, whiskers crisp as celery sprang from his cheeks, and his whole body sank low as a footstool and grew fur, nicely patterned in black and white like a tuxedo. His tail stood up straight as a wand.

He flicked the tail to get the feel of it. He bowed and stretched his paws and discovered his claws. They gleamed, then disappeared into the wonderful sheaths at the tip of each paw. Wrapped around a claw on his right paw, the thread of death might have been a dustball, a feather, a scrap of tweed.

Anatole scampered into the tailor's bedroom and bounded to the foot of the bed. He heard the trap door close. He tucked his paws under him and waited for the tailor to wake up.

The street noises began: cars passed the tailor's shop, a bus groaned and stopped, groaned and started. Women's voices drew near and faded away. The tailor sat up. He saw the cat at the foot of the bed, and his mouth fell open.

"Good morning," said Anatole.

"A talking cat! Mother of God!" cried the tailor.

He sprang out of bed and darted into the far corner of the bedroom. And wonder of wonders, right behind him danced twelve golden needles, and on the needles danced the golden cloak of Arcimboldo the Marvelous, and the needles were clacking away, for they never wasted a moment from the time the tailor opened his eyes to the time he closed them.

"Didn't you wish for a talking cat?" asked Anatole.

The tailor squeezed himself behind the nightstand, and what a strange figure he made, hugging himself in his nightshirt while the cloak gathered itself around him and the needles went on knitting, click, click, click.

"Think hard," said Anatole. "Didn't you wish for a talking cat? Because if there's been a mistake, I can go back where I came from."

Though the tailor was terribly frightened, he did not want to lose so rare a companion as a talking cat. He put his teeth in and adjusted them.

"I have often wished for a cat since my old cat died," said the tailor. "But I don't think I ever wished for a talking cat."

"I'm the deluxe model," said Anatole. "And I'll stay

with you and catch your mice and keep you company, on one condition."

"What condition?" asked the tailor.

"Never tell anyone I can talk."

"I won't tell a soul," said the tailor.

"And now," said Anatole, "if you'll be so kind as to bring me my breakfast."

"Of course," said the tailor.

And he bustled joyfully about the tiny kitchen, lit the gas burner, and set the table with two white porcelain bowls, one for himself and one for Anatole.

"Grape Nuts?" he asked. "My old cat loved Grape Nuts."

"I love Grape Nuts," said Anatole.

They ate in silence, the tailor leaning forward on his stool, drinking tea with one hand and stroking Anatole with the other. From deep inside Anatole rose a purr, which surprised him, for he did not know he was making it. He had a most unfamiliar urge to wash his face. The tailor poured himself tea from the porcelain pot and said, "I shall call you Pai Shan. All my cats are called Pai Shan. You are the fourth to carry that name."

"And I shall call you Noble Master," said Anatole, because it seemed the proper thing to do.

The tailor looked perfectly delighted.

"Noble Master," said Anatole, "I've never before seen needles that knit by themselves. I suppose you take great care of them."

"Great care," said the tailor. "A thief tried to steal them

"THEY ATE IN SILENCE, THE TAILOR LEANING FORWARD ON HIS STOOL, DRINKING TEA WITH ONE HAND AND STROKING ANATOLE WITH THE OTHER."

once, and they nearly killed him. No matter where I go, they stick by me. Watch."

He rose from the table and walked out of the kitchen into the workroom. The needles bobbed right after him, whisking the cloak behind them, and the clatter and clack of needle upon needle sounded like the grinding of teeth.

"They won't follow anyone else," the tailor said proudly.

"They are wonderful," said Anatole. "I suppose you got them from a great magician?"

"I got them from my father, who got them from his father, who was given them by the emperor of China, in exchange for making the empress's wedding gown."

"And where did the emperor get them?" inquired Anatole.

"Oh, that's a story," said the tailor, smiling. "When the emperor was an infant, his grandmother gave him a golden teething ring. When he grew up, he had all the teeth he wanted and no hope of cutting any more, so he had the ring melted down and forged into these needles."

The needles gathered themselves into a crown over the tailor's head, and the golden cloak slipped off and rolled down his shoulder in buttery waves.

"Is the cloak finished?" asked Anatole.

"All finished, and just in time," said the tailor. "Come, Delicious. Come, Winesap. Come, McIntosh, and Jonathan, and Rome Beauty. Come, Bonum and Fallawater and Yellow Newton and Fall Pippin and Russet and Northern Spy. Come, my most beautiful Gloria Mundi."

The tailor stroked Anatole between the ears.

"My father was fond of apples, but in China he seldom got any. In America he liked to buy apples at the fruit stand on Orchard Street. The apple man always said, 'What kind do you want?' And when my father learned how many different kinds of apples grow in America, he could only say, 'How wonderful apples are!' and he named his needles after the apples. 'The needles are wonderful,' he would say, 'and the apples are wonderful too.'"

Bang, bang, bang!

"It's the wizard come for his cloak," exclaimed the tailor, and he tossed the cloak on the counter and, followed by the twelve golden needles, ran into the bedroom to fetch his clothes. Anatole seized the end of the cloak in his claws. So strong is the thread of life that the cloak did not tear, but row by row, from the bottom up, it began to unravel, and it was half gone by the time the tailor returned, pulling his trousers over his nightshirt.

But the tailor was too excited to notice. He opened the door, and the first customer of the day strode into the room, shaking the snow off himself like a dog.

9.

He looked exactly as Anatole had seen him in the coffee shop on the first day of his visit: red hair, red beard, and hunched into the same fur coat. He drew the collar around his face and the owl shifted her weight on his arm as he leaned forward and inspected the golden cape with keen eyes.

"Did you use all the thread?" asked Arcimboldo.

"All the thread, dear Arcimboldo," replied the tailor.

"You didn't break it? You didn't cut it?"

"My needles always do as they're told," said the tailor. "Try it on."

Arcimboldo shook out the cloak. It was collared in glory but hemmed in a snarl of golden thread. The tailor began to tremble.

"Dear Arcimboldo, five minutes ago the cloak was done. I myself laid it on the table."

"Dear Cicero Yin," sneered Arcimboldo, "have you any idea who unraveled it?"

The tailor hung his head.

"Dear, dear Cicero Yin, believe me, things are bad for you. You have a pair of demons in your attic."

"Demons!" cried the tailor.

"My owl saw two demons fly into your attic last night. Watch out, Cicero Yin. Lock your trap door tonight. Because if my cloak isn't finished by tomorrow morning, I'll turn you into a carrot and eat you alive."

Terrified, the tailor bowed deeply.

"I'm most grateful to your owl for warning me of my great danger. Honorable owl, may I reward you for your services?"

"I'd like a plate of shrimp on rice cakes," said the owl. "Right now."

And she flew from Arcimboldo's arm to the tailor's shoulder, and all the time he was picking the shrimp out of the jar, she nagged him, "More! More!" and "Duck sauce, I want duck sauce!" and "Noodles, more noodles," till he had given away both his lunch and his supper. Nor did she so much as thank him for setting his own bowl, heaped with delicacies, before her on the counter.

The owl fluttered to the bowl and gobbled up the shrimp. Anatole, watching her, thought of Uncle Terrible upstairs, who was surely starved by this time. He thought of the treachery of the owl, first at Arcimboldo's house and now at the tailor's, and the next moment he leaped on her and sank his teeth into her wing.

"Grab the cat—he'll kill her!" shrieked Arcimboldo.

The tailor seized Anatole and shook him, and Anatole opened his jaws and let the owl drop. He had no intention of killing her, but he hoped to keep her from flying, and the sight of her torn wing brought a purr to his throat.

"There's your culprit," howled Arcimboldo. "There's your villain. There's the demon who unraveled my cloak."

And he stared long and hard at Anatole. With his skill in magic, he saw right off that this cat was enchanted. The eyes of enchanted animals are full of that odd mixture of pain and humor found only in the eyes of human beings, and they always shine with longing to return to themselves.

"Put that cat out tonight, Cicero Yin, if you want to live the rest of your life as man. Your word—give me your word on it."

"People say that a great blizzard is—"

"A cloak or a carrot," said Arcimboldo. "Choose."

"Dear Arcimboldo, I—"

The wizard was tucking the owl into his fur coat, which made him appear to have two heads, one large and one small.

"I give you my word," faltered the tailor.

The thinnest twist of a smile lit Arcimboldo's face as he opened the door and stalked out, leaving the tailor clutching the fragment of cloak while his golden needles danced overhead.

Through the open door came the voices of children passing:

"Hey, hey,
Can't catch me.
I'm sitting on top of
The Christmas tree."

The golden needles paused in midair. Then they rushed toward the open door. The tailor ran after them, and a snowball hit him in the chest.

"Move on, move on!" shouted the tailor, and he slammed the door.

But the children only sang louder.

"Liar, liar,
Your pants are on fire.
Your nose is as long
As a telephone wire."

Now the needles threw themselves at the door, pitifully, like children begging to go outside and join the others.

"They'll follow anyone who sings nonsense," groaned the tailor, wiping his forehead with the sleeve of his nightshirt. "They've never forgotten their days as a teething ring. Nonsense always reminds them of their youth, when they never knew a day of work."

Anatole was too astonished to speak. But the tailor, calmer now, took a tape measure from around his neck and measured the remnant of the golden cloak.

"If they work from now till tomorrow morning, they can finish the cloak. Now tell me, Pai Shan, did you unravel the golden thread?"

A helpful lie stood on the tip of his tongue, but Anatole remembered the spider's warning: *No one who lies or steals can command them.*

"I did."

"But would you do it again?"

"I might."

"Oh, Lord," said the tailor, sighing. "You'd better take the day off and sleep by the stove. You'll be cold enough tonight."

Anatole laid his head on his paws and dozed by the oven, but he did not sleep. He checked for the thread of death tied around his claws—it was quite safe. He listened to the tailor putting on his clothes and to the wind rising outside. When the wind dropped and the tailor shifted the position of the cloth, he heard, in the silence, the click-click of the golden needles, knitting the thread of life.

Presently he heard something else: a scratching behind the stove. He lifted his head and pricked up his ears. A brown mouse peeped out from behind the stove, caught Anatole's eye, and unfurled a white flag.

"Truce," it squeaked.

"Truce," said Anatole, who thought the mouse very cunning and would not have hurt it for the world.

Five more mice stepped out and bowed deeply.

"We hope," said the mouse holding the flag, "that for a suitable reward we may maintain our old pact."

"What pact?" asked Anatole.

"Our pact with the cats in this house. The last three cats always left us a tenth part of their supper behind the stove. We in turn promised to disturb nothing in the tailor's cupboards. Naturally, there is compensation." The mouse cleared its throat. "A selection of monthly premiums."

"Premiums?"

"The treasures of the hunt. Leif Langhal, show him the premiums."

A young mouse with a very long tail came forward, lugging a silver brooch wrought in the shape of three baby birds in a nest. Both birds and nest were pocked with holes.

"Real diamonds," said Leif Langhal.

"A YOUNG MOUSE WITH A VERY LONG TAIL CAME FORWARD,
LUGGING A SILVER BROOCH..."

"But they've all fallen out," said Anatole.

"You don't like the brooch?" exclaimed Leif Langhal, surprised. "We were sure you'd like the brooch. Cats generally like birds."

"Haven't you anything else?" asked Anatole.

The mice whispered among themselves for a few minutes, and Leif Langhal was heard to protest, "That's an awful lot of work," and the others whispered, "Sssssshh-hhh," and Leif Langhal said, "Well, hang it all, if I had a wagon to carry it in and a crane to lift it—" and the others pinched him till he squeaked, and the sewing machine stopped sewing. The tailor cocked his head—had he heard mice?

No. He heard nothing but the clack-clack of his faithful needles.

"Don't you have anything besides a brooch with the stones picked out?" asked Anatole.

"Only a book," said the mouse with the flag. "An old book that Leif picked up at the cockroaches' bazaar. We rarely trade with them. So much of their merchandise is enchanted. But the book can't harm any of us, for of course we can't read. It's very handsome. An addition to any shelf. Here comes Leif—see for yourself."

Anatole could scarcely believe his eyes. In his paws, Leif was dragging Uncle Terrible's magic book.

"I agree to the pact," said Anatole. "On one condition."

The mice exchanged uneasy glances.

"The trap door in the ceiling of the workroom will be

locked tonight. Do you know another way up to the room?"

"Yes, indeed," said a plump gray mouse. "There are three passages leading directly to the loft."

"But they're blocked with plaster," said Leif Langhal, "and we'll have to clear one. That's an awful lot of work."

"How long will it take to clear one?" asked Anatole.

"We could finish it by midnight, I think," said the gray mouse.

"Listen, brothers," said Anatole. "A friend of mine is hiding in that loft. I want you to take him this book and bring him here. Tell him that the golden needles will follow anyone who sings nonsense. And show him how to find the Grape Nuts and the tea. He never skips breakfast, and he hasn't eaten for ages."

"Is your friend a mouse?" asked Leif Langhal.

"No, he's even bigger than the tailor. But very soon he will be no taller than yourselves."

The tailor pushed back his chair, and the mice slipped behind the stove.

"Remember," murmured a voice, light as a baby's breathing, "the tenth part of your supper. To be left behind the stove."

"I'll remember," said Anatole.

That evening the tailor ate no supper. He sat at his kitchen table, the tears running down his face, with Anatole on his lap, and he fed Anatole bites of cold chicken from his own hand, saying, "Take a little more, dear Pai Shan. Take a little more."

Beside them, the tailor's old radio sputtered the seven-o'clock news. The news was all weather: "Snow will continue into the evening—crackle, crackle. It's ten below in the city, temperature falling fast—crackle—windy and colder tonight. Arctic winds of fifty miles an hour are blowing this way from the northwest. Twenty-three inches of snow predicted—"

The tailor snapped it off.

"You're putting me outside in winds of fifty miles an hour?" cried Anatole.

The tailor whisked out his handkerchief and blew his nose. "I'll give you my scarf and a box to creep into—I'll give you a box—"

And he hurried into the workroom to find a box. Soon Anatole heard a great pounding. The tailor was nailing the trap door shut. Anatole put his nose to the place where the stove met the wall and called softly, "Leif!"

Silence. At last a small voice answered him.

"What do you want?"

"I have an important errand for you. Come out."

Leif Langhal appeared, looking rather sleepy and a little frightened. "What's the errand?"

"Do you know where Himmel Hill is?"

"All animals know where Himmel Hill is."

"And Mother's house? Do you know how to find it?"

"Don't *you* know how to find it? We're born knowing that."

"I need somebody to carry a message to Mother—

somebody with wings. I need somebody who can fly to Mother's house and tell everybody in it to come here right away."

Leif stared at him, stupefied.

"Find me somebody to carry this message," pleaded Anatole, "and I shall ask my friend in the loft to give you a . . . a pound of Cheddar cheese."

"A pound!" squeaked Leif Langhal. "Why, so much cheese would not fit through our door. We would have to chop it into a great many pieces, and that would be an awful lot of work."

"Half a pound then," said Anatole. "And I'll chop it up for you."

Leif Langhal closed his eyes for so long that Anatole feared he was falling asleep.

"I know a dove," Leif Langhal said in a dreamy voice. "She lives in a dovecote on a roof not far from here. But she wouldn't go out tonight. Not in this weather."

Through Anatole's head flashed the dovecote in the garden at the top of the fire escape. How desolate the rooftop must look now, the flowers dead under the snow, the grape arbor a white tunnel.

"The starling," murmured a voice. "Ask the starling who lives in the ventilation shaft."

Behind Leif Langhal appeared the plump gray mouse.

"Wait in the alley by the back door tonight," said the gray mouse. "We'll call the starling."

A footfall sent the two mice scurrying for shelter. The

tailor stooped and picked up Anatole, stroked him behind the ears, tied his own scarf around his neck, and carried him tenderly to the front door.

"I've made a box for you outside," said the tailor. "Forgive me, Pai Shan. Please forgive me."

The door closed behind him, and as if it had been lying in wait for him all this time, the wind charged at Anatole full force. The box that the tailor had set out, lined with his own pillow, hurtled itself down the street just as though it were running away, and the tailor's scarf unwound itself from Anatole's neck and writhed into the air and vanished in a swirl of snow. Already the cars and the fire hydrant had the heavy shapelessness of clay things made by a beginner. Ice crystallized at the edge of his fur. He had not known ice could be so heavy or so cold.

By the time he reached the back door, he could scarcely breathe. Then a chillier thought struck him: tomorrow, in the first light of morning, he would be a child once more. A child in sneakers and a denim jacket. If Mother did not come, he would certainly freeze to death with the thread of death in his hand. And if he called for help, who over the howling of the wind could hear him?

Huddled in the alley, he dreamed himself in front of the fireplace at home after his bath, and part of him thought how much he would love a hot bath—that was the child part of him—and part of him thought, Could anything be worse than a hot bath? That was the cat part of him, and so he dreamed this way and that, now want-

ing one thing, now the other, till a voice at his ear roused
him: "He can't go."

Anatole opened his eyes. By the back door, through a
chink between the bricks, peeped Leif Langhal.

"Who can't go?"

"The starling. We found him on the roof, frozen to
death."

"There must be somebody who can go," cried Anatole.

"There is," said the mouse, "but she's not very reli-
able. She lives in the loft."

"A bird?" asked Anatole.

"A bat," said the mouse. "But she's awfully dopey.
They're always like that when they're hibernating. And
she's never seen snow before."

"Where is she?" asked Anatole.

The mouse pointed straight up. On the rail of the upstairs porch hung a fat black pear, blowing in the wind.

"Can she carry a message?" Anatole asked doubtfully.

"She's very educated," said the mouse, "but at this
time of the year she's a little queer in the head."

"Better her than no one," said Anatole. "Dear bat,
come down."

"Don't call her down," warned the mouse. "She can't
take off from the ground."

Anatole trudged up the stairs to the porch, and each
stair froze his paws with a slick of ice hidden under the
hummock of snow. Putting his mouth close to the bat's
ear, Anatole shouted, "Can you hear me?"

"Um," said the bat, screwing up her face.

"I want you to fly to Himmel Hill. I want you to find Mother and the invisible girl. Tell the girl to bring her skip rope, and tell Mother and all the animals to come at once. And hurry."

"Give me room," muttered the bat in a thick voice.

She dropped from the railing, as if she had lost her grasp, but just before she hit the snow she swooped up and circled the roof twice.

"Go east!" called Anatole.

"I can only fly in circles," the bat called back. "But if I make my circles big enough"—the wind howled, and her voice grew very faint—"I shall certainly find—"

A gust of snow carried her off, and she was lost to sight.

The bat could see nothing but snow. This did not alarm her, however, for she was listening to the humming in the great still place all animals carry deep inside them that shows them their way over the most baffling distances. Birds and butterflies flying south, whales moving to warmer waters, stray dogs hunting for home—it is Mother's humming they listen for. If they make a wrong turn, they can scarcely hear it at all, and then they know they must turn another way. The bat heard it loud and clear, and she knew she could find Mother's house well enough.

But what of the wind that iced her wings? Mother

could do nothing about that. From her childhood in a belfry, listening to sermons, the bat knew a great many proverbs, and in trying situations she recited them to herself, to keep up her spirits.

"A rolling bone gathers no sauce," murmured the bat. It did not sound quite right. "A bowling scone bathers no dross. No—A rolling stone gathers no moss. Now that's right," she told herself triumphantly, and pleased with her success, she tried another. "It's a shrill finned that throws no good. No—It's an ill wind that blows no good. Ah, in warm weather, on a summer's night I can say hundreds of them without missing a syllable. But in winter, when half of me is asleep, what can I expect?"

From far off she spied the rutabaga lamp. It shone amber in the window of Mother's room, as it always shines for those who look for it. She dipped low and glided toward it. The window opened, and she blew in and sank by the fire, exhausted.

Near her, by a well, sat a mole. And near the mole a rope was spinning round and round, and the thump, thump that the rope made when it struck the floor might have been the heartbeat of the invisible jumper that turned it.

"I have something to deliver," said the bat, panting a little.

Rosemarie stopped skipping, the rope fell to the floor, the mole sat up attentively.

"Oranges," said the bat. "It might have been oranges."

"Oranges?" repeated Rosemarie, and she picked up

the bat, brought it close to the fire, and stroked it. The bat showed no surprise at being held by someone she could not see; there was so much in the world that she could not see with her weak eyes.

"Or lemons," murmured the bat.

"You don't remember what you came to deliver?" asked the mole.

"Eggs?" suggested Rosemarie. She tried to think of things that people might want delivered. "Newspapers? Milk?"

"Moss?" asked the mole.

"Or mail? Or messages?" asked Rosemarie.

"A message!" exclaimed the bat. "It's a message. And a very important message," she added. "Sell the churl to spring her flip soap and sell all the maminuls to chum at punce. And furry."

An astonished silence greeted this speech.

"That's the message?" said the mole.

"That's the gist of it," said the bat. "I may have got a few things scrambled."

"Could you say the message again?" asked Rosemarie. "We'll try to listen more carefully."

The bat closed her eyes. "Fell the burl to fling her pip pope and swell all the fainifuls to pum at dunce. And purry."

"Who sent you?" said Rosemarie.

"A mouse," replied the bat, "and a cat."

"Where did you meet this mouse and this cat?" asked Rosemarie.

"At the house of the skin-changer."

By this name are all tailors known to all bats, but the mole knew it too, for he had close friends among the bats.

"The tailor," said the mole. "She means the tailor."

"I've got it, I've got it," exclaimed the bat. "Tell the girl to bring her skip rope and tell all the animals to come at once. And hurry."

"Call Mother," said the mole. "Call the creatures."

That night the snow sprinkled the city with silence. It buried the bus stops, it built hummocks over the parked cars, it heaped hills over the entrances to the subways. Coffee houses, drugstores, butcher shops, bars closed down, and all the bustle and traffic of the city ceased.

Through the snowswept city moved the animals, padding, galloping, loping, flying, darting. Snow brushed their footprints and hushed their hoofbeats, and Mother marched behind them, the flames on her antlers beaming a path.

They passed the fish store. They passed the Ebony Beauty Parlor. At the dark door of Cicero Yin, the creatures stopped and huddled together. Half buried in the snow, which covered his stoop, a child's hand and a pair of feet poked out.

"Sneakers," clucked Mother, "in this weather."

"Oh, Mother, it's Anatole," cried Rosemarie, "and he's dead!"

"THE CREATURES CROWDED AROUND HIM, AND THOSE IN FRONT
LICKED THE SNOW ASIDE..."

The creatures crowded around him, and those in front licked the snow aside, and when his denim jacket appeared and then his face, so still and so pale, they bellowed and mewed and barked and howled, till Mother pushed her way past them. She didn't weep, not she. She folded her arms over her chest and said severely, "Anatole, didn't I tell you to wear your boots? Didn't I tell you to button your jacket?"

And she picked him up in her arms and blew on his face, his hands, his feet. A faint flush came into them. He moved first one leg, then the other. When he opened his eyes, Mother set him on his feet. Everyone cheered.

"How cold I am," he whispered. "Mother, open the door."

Mother bowed her head, and the golden light her antlers threw on the door seemed to melt its heart. The lock sprang open with a sigh, the door opened, and the animals trooped in.

Uncle Terrible was dancing around the room in the golden cloak while the bare needles clapped over his head, and now he ran joyfully to meet them.

"The cloak of life is finished," he exclaimed. "But the cloak of death is not yet started. We'll rhyme those needles to work. They'll do anything for a bit of nonsense."

Anatole slid the thread of death from his finger and sang:

> "Mother, Mother, I am ill.
> Send for the doctor on the hill.

Doctor, doctor, will I die?
Yes, my dear, and so must I."

To the delight of everyone, the twelve golden needles danced forward, hooked themselves to the thread, and started to knit.

In his bedroom, the tailor slept and dreamed. He dreamed that Arcimboldo the Marvelous was chasing him with a vegetable parer and shouting at him, louder and louder, till he shouted so loud that the tailor woke up.

"What do I hear?" he said to himself.

Not shouting. No. A thump, thump, thump like the tread of an enormous animal, accompanied by a chorus of queer voices, some cracked, some shrill, some deep, all joyful:

"How many years will I live?
One, two, three, four, five, six—"

Much alarmed, the tailor jumped out of bed, popped in his teeth, and pulled on his trousers. As he hurried to the door of his workroom, he met a troop of mice, and every mouse was skipping a rope cut from his own threads. When he arrived at the threshold, the tailor could scarcely believe his eyes. A giantess and a boy and a man and a great crowd of animals were skipping rope, and the ropes were all made of tweeds and twills and gabardines, and in the middle of the room, one rope— one *real* rope—was spinning faster than the rest around thin air. The golden needles were dancing themselves into a blur like spun honey. And while he watched, open-mouthed, a magnificent silver cloak floated from the needles to the floor in shimmering folds.

Before the tailor could ask any questions, a girl with long black braids and wearing a nightgown popped out of nowhere, right into the fastest rope, and the raccoon shouted, "Why, you're human!" and everybody else whooped and hollered.

"It's finished, the cloaks are finished!"

Mother gathered them up, the golden cloak on her right arm, the silver on her left.

"Make peace, you two," she said, and she tossed them into the air, and they stuck together as one fabric, and Mother threw it over her shoulders, just as a loud knocking shook the front door.

Everyone froze.

"It's Arcimboldo!" shrieked the tailor. "Give me that cloak, madam."

He tugged at it in vain. Mother towered over him like a tree.

"Don't be afraid, Cicero Yin. Anatole will settle with Arcimboldo, and I shall pull a little wool over his eyes. When he comes in, he'll see nobody but a young stranger behind the counter."

Bang, bang, bang.

"Open the door, Cicero Yin!"

Mother leaned over Anatole, laid the snakeskin on his shoulders, and put Uncle Terrible's magic book in his hand.

"Tell him the door is open. Don't forget to show him the book."

"The door is open, Arcimboldo," said Anatole, all a-tremble. "Come in."

Arcimboldo burst into the room, and Mother took from the pocket of her apron a handful of snow—and yet not snow, for real snow quickly melts in your pocket—and she flung it at the wizard and at the owl who rode on his shoulder. Anatole noted with satisfaction a Band-Aid on her wing.

"Where's the tailor?" roared Arcimboldo, and he pounded his fist on the counter.

"Yes, where's the tailor?" sneered the owl.

The tailor stood not four feet from both of them, quaking and shaking. The animals did not move; from hunting and being hunted, they knew how to remain perfectly still.

"I'm his helper," said Anatole. "Can I help you?"

"I've come for my cloak."

"For his cloak," croaked the bird.

"Can you wait just a minute?" asked Anatole.

"One minute." Arcimboldo drew out his pocket watch, and the death's-head engraved on the back winked at Anatole. "It is one minute of eight. At eight o'clock I keep my promise to the tailor, wherever he is. A carrot, a carrot."

Tick, tick, tick.

"The tailor says you're a wise man," said Anatole. "Now, I have a book here that I can't read."

"You can't read?" snapped the wizard. "Dumbbell."

"It's written in a foreign language," said Anatole. "The tailor says you know all languages. But I'll bet you don't know this one."

"Let's have a look," said the wizard.

He picked up the book and held it at arm's length, and Anatole quietly raised the flowers over the page while Arcimboldo read,

"Woneka, wonodo,
Eka mathaka rata—"

The owl spied a spill of Grape Nuts on the counter—Uncle Terrible had finished off the box—and she flew to the feast.

"A gbae se
Dombra, dombra, dombra."

Suddenly the lean figure of Arcimboldo disappeared. But on the counter, in front of Anatole, a very tiny Arcimboldo was shaking his fists and hopping up and down, knee-deep in the Grape Nuts.

Everyone was too astonished to move or speak, except the owl, who was so absorbed in her eating that she did not even look up. But she was heard to say, with immense satisfaction, "At last—a really fine mouse."

And before anyone could stop her, she plucked up Arcimboldo in her beak and ate him.

Then she too disappeared. And there in the shop stood

the lady from Brooklyn in her curly fur coat, just as Anatole remembered her from the coffee shop. Finding herself transported to the tailor's shop in her bare feet, she looked about in bewilderment.

Outside, on every side, bells were ringing as if all the bells in the city were celebrating a great victory.

"The last spell is broken," said Mother. "The bells are saying good-bye and fading into air. The prisoners of the bells are free. They are waking up in the places they left behind them. And the people who gave them up for lost are saying to one another, 'It's a miracle.'"

"Am I dreaming?" asked the woman from Brooklyn.

Mother laughed. "No. But as the sun climbs higher, you will forget this night, though many nights have passed in my country during this single night in yours. First you will forget Arcimboldo. Then you will forget Anatole and his friends. Last of all, you will forget me. You, dear lady, and you, Cicero, will say to yourselves, 'What a wonderful dream I had! If only I could remember it.' That is how it feels to come out of an enchantment."

"I hope I never forget you," said Anatole.

"Not everyone forgets me," said Mother.

The bells grew fainter and fainter and died away altogether. Mother tucked the magic book into her apron pocket and tied the snakeskin around her waist.

"You won't mind my taking these things, Uncle Terrible?"

"It's the least I can do for you," said Uncle Terrible, who was only too glad to be rid of them.

"Children," said Mother, "it is time to go home. My floor wants sweeping, and my lamp must be put to sleep at sunrise. My creatures know the way to my house. But Anatole and Rosemarie and Uncle Terrible shall ride with me on my cloak."

"Are they going to Himmel Hill?" asked the raccoon, who did not want to leave Rosemarie.

"Not this time," said Mother. "Are you ready, Anatole? And Rosemarie? And Uncle Terrible?"

"Pardon me," squeaked a tiny voice, "but there was a promise of Cheddar."

A single leap carried Leif Langhal into the palm of Mother's hand.

"A cat whose face I do not see here promised us half a pound of Cheddar chopped into pieces for easy transport, in exchange for our services, faithfully rendered."

"Of course," said Mother.

She lifted her free hand, and a wheel of Cheddar dropped out and bounced toward the kitchen, pausing only long enough to break into twenty smaller wheels that rolled behind the stove and straight into the mousehole.

"All these marvels have exhausted me," said the bat. "If you'll excuse me, I'm going back to bed. Where is my bed?"

"Up there," said Mother, pointing to the trap door. Instantly the nails that closed it snapped in two. The door opened, and the bat flew straight up into the loft.

"Cicero Yin, the lady from Brooklyn wants the dress

you promised her. What an eager customer, to come so early!"

As Mother spoke, she unfurled her cape, the golden side up. It fluttered behind her on some secret breeze of its own.

"Get on board, children," sang Mother.

Anatole and Rosemarie climbed on. But Uncle Terrible hesitated, fearing that so frail a fabric could not possible hold him.

"Don't worry, Uncle Terrible." Mother laughed. "There's room for many more."

It was an invitation he could not refuse. And when he had settled himself comfortably on the cape, with the two children on his lap, Mother opened the door of the shop.

She raised her hand and sent a single beam of light spinning through the dark like a ribbon of amber.

"There's your road, my darlings. Take care."

Anatole could not see the animals as they raced along the road. The light dissolved both their shapes and their shadows. But he could hear them barking and roaring and squeaking and thumping, and he heard the mole singing at the top of his voice,

> "The least of Mother's errands
> Is good enough for me,"

just as Mother rose into the air and soared, as slow and grand as a cloud, over the rooftops of the city.

Then her cloak billowed up and covered them.

"...MOTHER ROSE INTO THE AIR AND SOARED,
AS SLOW AND GRAND AS A CLOUD..."

IO.

ncle Terrible, we're home!"

She had set them down in Uncle Terrible's living room, beside the little house. The kitchen was swept and the table cleared. Anatole knew this was Mother's work, for she could not bear an untidy house.

Uncle Terrible rushed about, crowing for joy. "Here's my King Kong, and my Statue of Liberty, and, oh, here are my comics, safe and sound!"

He scooped up a *Superman* comic from the closet. On

"SHE HAD SET THEM DOWN IN UNCLE TERRIBLE'S LIVING ROOM,
BESIDE THE LITTLE HOUSE."

the cover, how tiny and bright and flat Superman looked as he leaped tall buildings with a single bound.

"I think we're the real superheroes," said Anatole.

"I think we are too," said Uncle Terrible.

From overhead they both heard it: thump, thump, thump.

"Can we invite Rosemarie to play with the little house?" asked Anatole.

"Of course," said Uncle Terrible.

"I'll call her right away," said Anatole.

He climbed out on the fire escape. An orange light crept into the sky. Already the snow on the steps was melting. He ran up the steps two at a time.

When he reached the top, he looked down. Below him lay the church and the schoolyard, and higher and beyond, the television antennas that covered the rooftops like dead trees. Arcimboldo's trees, he thought. How long ago it all seemed to him now!

Far off gleamed the river. A train slipped past like a silver snake. The white turrets of Himmel Hill pricked the pale darkness, but a single light winked and flickered in the midst of them like a friendly star.

"Mother is putting her lamp to sleep," said Anatole, and he waved, just as the sun burst out of hiding and covered the lovely world at his feet with gold.

NANCY WILLARD (1936–2017) was a prolific author of seventy books of poems and fiction for adults and children. In 1982, her picture book *A Visit to William Blake's Inn: Poems for Innocent and Experienced Travelers* was the first book of poems to win the Newbery Medal and was awarded a Caldecott Honor for illustrations by Alice and Martin Provensen. She taught literature at Vassar College from 1965 until she retired in 2013.

DAVID McPHAIL was born in Newburyport, Massachusetts, and attended the School of the Museum of Fine Arts in Boston. He has written and/or illustrated more than a hundred books.

TITLES IN SERIES

EILÍS DILLON
The Island of Horses

PENELOPE FARMER
Charlotte Sometimes

RUMER GODDEN
An Episode of Sparrows

RICHARD WARREN HATCH
The Curious Lobster
Illustrated by Marion Freeman Wakeman

NORMAN LINDSAY
The Magic Pudding

ERIC LINKLATER
The Wind on the Moon
Illustrated by Nicolas Bentley

J. P. MARTIN
Uncle
Illustrated by Quentin Blake

JEAN MERRILL
The Pushcart War
Illustrated by Ronni Solbert

DANIEL PINKWATER
Lizard Music

MARGERY SHARP
The Rescuers
Illustrated by Garth Williams

BARBARA SLEIGH
Carbonel: The King of the Cats

T. H. WHITE
Mistress Masham's Repose
Illustrated by Fritz Eichenberg